The Prey

Jolene Morrey

Contents

Chapter 1: Captured

"There's a vampire!" I whisper-shout. "The candle!" I whip away from the crack in the barn wall and lunge for the light that's about to give away our position. After walking for the entire day, this old abandoned barn seemed like the perfect place to take shelter for the night. Now that candle is acting as a beacon, shining through the cracks in the wall and drawing in the very creatures we are trying to escape.

A large figure blocks my path to the candle, bouncing me back as I crash into his hard chest. I lose my balance and fall back onto the dirt and straw that covers the barn floor.

"Not so fast, girl," Neil says, blocking the candle. "Is he alone?"

"Are you crazy? That light will be the death of us," I say.

"Is he alone?" he repeats, slower. My heart is beating through my chest. It's dark outside, and the vampire will spot the light at any second. Does he want us all to die?

"It's just him and his horse. Now put it out, quick."

He glances at the other two men, and his lips curl up into a grin. He gives a small nod. The one unsheathes his sword, and the other picks up his bow.

My face goes pale. "No. It's suicide. We need to stay hidden and wait for him to pass. This shoddy barn looks abandoned. He won't know we're here."

Neil steps around me, and the three men gather by the large barn door. "We will not lie down and let those vile monsters take our country," he says.

"What are you talking about? They've already taken it. We've lost. Escaping to Faria is our only chance now."

Neil tries to get a glimpse of the vampire through a crack in the wall. "Listen, farmhand, if we want your advice on matters of war, we'll ask."

I get back on my feet and dust the hay off my pants. "My name's not farmhand, it's Julia, and you're stonemasons, not soldiers."

The men look at each other and give one last nod. The blond man kicks open the door, and they burst out the barn while shouting their battle cry. I run to the door and slam it closed, then I bolt back to the candle and smother it in the dirt.

A blood chilling scream sends a shiver down my spine. I hurry back to the wall and look through a crack between two wooden planks. Another agonizing wail follows. I can't see them. I jerk my head around the crack, trying to find an angle. In my heart, I want to scream for them to run, to just escape. The vampire may have mercy on injured men running in fear, but my breath sticks in my throat. If I scream, if I draw attention to this barn, then the vampire will come for me.

"No, no, no, please!" a man begs. It's Neil. My stomach flips. Ever since we fled from our village, he's been the leader of our little group of four. His unwavering confidence that we would all make it to Faria is what kept my fear at bay. This can't be happening. Neil never panics.

Another wail follows, but it's cut short. I stumble backwards and struggle to keep my footing. He's dead. They're dead. They're all dead.

We were meant to run from the foreign vampire army, not fight them. I fled my village, leaving the only home I've ever known, leaving every person I grew up with to escape the violence, and now my traveling companions lie dead on the other side of the barn wall, with their murderer still lurking.

Why did he come for us? Why couldn't he leave us alone? What did Neil and the others even die for? We abandoned everything we had, lost everything we'd built up over our whole lives just to escape these creatures. There are no houses left for them to ransack, no treasures to be stolen or land to be taken. Yet the vampire came all this way just to kill us? We are nobodies.

I hear his footsteps. He's coming. My eyes dart around the barn. Hay, feeding troughs, buckets, blankets, lanterns, candles, everything but weapons, which are now all sprawled out outside. There's nothing left to defend myself. He's going to kill me.

I can't breathe. My lungs can't get enough air. I'm panicking. There's no one left but me. My thin linen clothes won't protect my skin from a sharp sword or my bones from a heavy mace. The vampire is going to come in here and murder me with his iron weapon. Neil's begging did nothing to quell the vampire's intent to take lives, and it'll be no different for me. I'll writhe in agony under the vampire's weapons for a few minutes before my bleeding body can no longer keep me alive. My brother will be left waiting for me in Faria, wondering where I am, and all that will be left of me is a still unburied corpse in an abandoned barn.

I hold my shaking hand and force myself to think straight, the force of my grip turning my fingers white. The barn's big, but there's only one door, and it leads straight to the vampire. I didn't scream or shout, so he doesn't know I'm here. I need to hide.

I grab a blanket and hurry to the darkest corner of the barn. Curling up beside a pile of hay, I cover myself with the coarse material, nestling into the hay to try disguise my body's shape. I brush stalks and straws over the blanket in an attempt to make it appear undisturbed.

The door swings open, and I freeze. My hand zips back under the blanket, and I lie dead still.

Heavy boots take slow steps on the opposite side of the room. He's among our clothes, food and supplies. Though I can't see anything under the dark blanket, I resist the urge to shut my eyes. I need to be ready to dash if he rips away the blanket.

While I might be dreading this moment, I know that the vampire will leave. My brother, Jacob, is waiting for me in Faria. He'll wrap me up in a hug, and we'll never be separated again. I'll cherish him even more than before. Despite all the hardship we've lived through, we still have each other. It'll be no different after this, this moment where I'm hiding from a murderous vampire on the hunt will be nothing more than a bad memory, a day I can forget.

The hay pricks at my bare arms and the small of my back, right where my shirt fails to meet my pants. I resist the urge to pull it down. Any movement will lead him to find me, and if I want to survive, he can't know that I'm here.

The vampire's footsteps stop. It's dead quiet, like he vanished into thin air. Did I move? Has he stopped to stare at the blanket?

A metal clank on the far side of the barn breaks the silence. I breathe again, but a shiver runs through my bones. He's got the lantern. He strikes the lighter stones together. The room lights up with a warm glow, and my blood runs cold.

The footsteps start again, but louder, followed by the creaking metal lantern in his hand. He's getting closer, and he has a light. Bright rays poke through the blanket's weaving, moving with him. I can hear my own breathing, and I pray he can't. My body is screaming to make a run for it, but I know that my best chance is to stay still, to act like I don't exist.

The footsteps stop, and the awful silence returns. He's close. He's very close. This blanket is the only thing between us. My whole body is trembling. When he's walking, his heavy steps beat fear into me, reminding me that a huge foreign warrior is only feet away, but his silence is even worse. I don't know what he's doing. He could be staring at me right now, amused at my pathetic attempt to hide.

The silence is eating away at me. What will it matter if he leaves the human hiding in the straw? I haven't wronged him or spat on his family name. I'm not a soldier. Ignoring my little life won't hinder their plan to conquer this country.

Just leave. Just leave. Just leave.

A hard boot strikes my leg, and a small cry escapes my lips. He rips the blanket away. The lantern's light exposes my trembling form, coming at me from every direction like a flock of vultures. I scramble away from the vampire standing over me, my hands slipping and sliding over the dirt and straw as I struggle to sit up. My stomach twists, bringing a wave of nausea.

There's a blood-stained sword just inches from my face. I continue to back away in a frantic panic. The bloody blade follows me, coming closer and closer. It creeps up on me like a predator with its own mind. My back hits the wall, and the blade presses against my chest. The tip pokes through my shirt and into my skin, drawing blood and making me wince. I can't breathe without deepening the cut.

The blade is short and curved, halfway between a sickle and a sword. I've never seen anything like it. It's not the weapon of a soldier, but a demon. My eyes follow the blade up to the figure holding it. He's pale, like a corpse, but his blood red eyes tell me he's very much alive. He looks to be in his late twenties, a decade older than me. Coal black hair covers his head, and he wears a long coat and a high-collared black cape marked with tinges of red – possibly blood.

I slowly open my hands, holding them up for him to see. I'm unarmed. I'm not a soldier. I'm a farmer. Don't kill me.

A smirk flashes in the corner of his lips. He's amused? My hands are shaking, and my heart feels like it's about to break out of my chest. This is the most terrible, terrifying moment of my life, and he finds it funny?

He retracts his sword and slides it back into the sheath on his belt. I can breathe again.

My eyes jump to the wide-open barn door – my gateway to safety. The vampire's a few feet away from me. This is my chance. I jump to my feet and lunge for the door.

The vampire's fist slams into my head, and my world goes spinning.

The next thing I know, my face is against the dirt and my ears are ringing. The ground moves beneath me. He's pulling me by my feet. I curl my arms around my head as a shield from the dirt.

The lightheadedness morphs into a searing headache. He's going to kill me. I've only just turned eighteen, and my life is going to end right as it began. My hands ball up into tight fists. This isn't fair. Why do I have to die when I've barely had a chance to live? I did everything

I could to escape death at a vampire's hand, yet it's coming for me anyway. Was I supposed to grab a stick and join Neil in his hopeless charge? Was I supposed to trek through the wilderness alone to reach Faria when I've never been further than a day's walk from our village?

The dirt and gravel scuff my shirt as he hauls my limp body outside. The moment he releases me, I scram to push myself up on all fours.

A heavy boot stomps on my back, slamming my body back into the ground and knocking the air out of my lungs. A warm burning pain crawls through my diaphragm. His boot remains on the center of my back, the pressure forcing me to take quick shallow breaths. I can't get away. I can't even crawl.

There's a moment of relief from the pressure as his boot disappears, but the knee that replaces it is even worse. I open my mouth to scream from the pain, but nothing comes out. I can't breathe. My arms flail about as I scramble to get away, but he yanks them up high behind my back, twisting them so it hurts to move. I shut my eyes and grit my teeth, giving up on any attempt to struggle away from him in a desperate hope to minimize the pain.

He ties a rope around one wrist, then the immense pressure disappears. I gasp for air. He pulls me up by the back of my shirt and forces my aching body against a tree.

Before I can react, he yanks on the rope, pulling my wrist behind my back and against the bark. He forces my arms backwards around the trunk and ties my wrists together, making me stand with my back flush against the tree.

I'm trapped. He takes a step back, looking pleased with his work. It all happened so fast that I didn't even have a chance to gather my bearings. They really are superhuman.

I stare at him with wide eyes, the hair on the back of my neck standing straight. He dwarfs me. The top of my tiny frame barely reaches his shoulders. My muscles are twitching in fear – my body's instinctual response to being at the mercy of a predator – but the tight bindings hold my arms still.

I avert my eyes, hoping to ignore his intimidating stature. What difference does it make if I block out the world now? He's engineered the situation so that I have no chance of getting away from him. Despite my body's desperate attempts to protect myself, there is absolutely nothing I can do. What good is a racing heart when my muscles can't move an inch? I shut my eyes and try to recall my fantasy about reuniting with Jacob at Faria. If this horrid reality is my end, I want my mind to be as far away from it as possible.

The vampire's rough hand grabs my chin and forces my head up. My disheveled blonde hair covers my eyes, but he brushes it aside. On instinct, my arms tug against the ropes to try protect my face, but it's fruitless. My eyes stay shut and my body trembles. I can't defend myself. I've never in all my life had someone grip my chin as if it was a handle. Having such a strong grip so close to my eyes is so foreign and intrusive that it anchors me to the moment, preventing my mind from going anywhere else. Every muscle in my face goes tense, expecting to be struck at any second.

To my relief, he releases my chin. I turn my head to the side and twist away from him. He places both hands under my arms, grips my sides and presses his thumbs into my chest. I wince and whimper under the pressure.

He moves his hands down a few inches, then presses both thumbs into my breasts. It hurts. I wish I was somewhere else, anywhere else, not at the mercy of this monster. I wish the ground would open up and swallow me, take me away from this terrible moment.

He releases his clamping hands, only to press in again just a few inches lower. He repeats the motion around my stomach, compressing my abdomen to half the size it's supposed to be. My body strains, and I groan. He'll crush me if he squeezes any harder, and I'm helpless to stop him. It's sore and intrusive. Please let this be the worst of it.

He moves his hands down my legs, pressing into my flesh every few inches, then he runs his finger between my shoes and ankles. The whole ordeal is over in a matter of minutes, but it felt like hours.

He unsheathes his blade, and I suddenly wish that he'd go back to poking me. He's going to cut me while I can't move? To torture me? I start to panic again. "No, no, no." I yank on the restraints, and the rope bites into my skin. I pull and pull and try to shuffle away from him.

He presses the blade against my neck, and I freeze.

"Fearful," he says.

I catch a glimpse of his freakishly long canines. The edge of the blade digs into my skin, just enough not to draw blood. He's precision puts me even more on edge. I stay still and silent, terrified that the slightest movement will lead the blade to gash me.

He turns away. I follow his trail with my eyes, and the sight ahead makes me sick. Neil and his two companions lie still in pools of blood.

He steps over their corpses, making his way to his black horse laying on the ground. It's dead too. He ruffles around in the saddle bag and pulls out a metal flask and a glass vial filled with a murky liquid.

He hacks at Neil's lifeless body with his blade, and I cringe at the sound of bones cracking.

He steps out of the way, and I have to shut my eyes to avoid getting sick. The image is burned into my mind. He cut out Neil's eyes.

Moving to the corpse of the blond-haired man, he repeats the procedure. I can't watch. There's more snapping and cutting as he does the same to the third man, and a plop as he drops the bloody eyeball into the flask.

He approaches my tree, with the bloody blade in one hand and the flask in the other.

"No, no, no, no," I choke out. "Let me go. Please let me go." Surely he wouldn't subject a living person to that?

He wipes the flat edge of the blade against my pants, cleaning it.

"Can you comprehend why I bound you?" he asks, seemingly unfazed by any of this. His carefree tone makes me shudder. Despite my distress, he couldn't be more comfortable. Is he drawing out the moment before my death for his own entertainment?

I shake my head, too afraid to attempt to answer him.

"So your little mind proposed that my purpose was to release you only a moment later?"

I shake my head again, not just saying no to his question but to this whole situation. I don't want to be tied up, I don't want to know why he tied me up, and I don't want to die like the others. "Please let me go," I whisper, "I didn't do anything."

He steps closer, his chest just a few inches from my face. His fingers brush my hair behind my ear, and he leans in.

His breath rolls over my neck. I tuck my head into my shoulder, as much as the rope allows, pressing as far away from him as I can. It's just to scare me, it's just to scare me, I repeat over and over in my mind, but he doesn't back off. He's sniffing me.

He swoops down, and I cry out from the sharp pain at the base of my neck. His fangs have punctured my skin. I try wiggle away, but his teeth only cut deeper into my flesh.

A warm liquid runs down my chest. His teeth stab me a second time, and I let out another scream. He's drinking my blood. I shut my eyes, staying as still as I can in the hope that he won't readjust his fangs again.

"Please stop, please."

His cold lips press against my collarbone.

The minutes pass, and he keeps drinking. My heart beats faster and faster, and I can't get enough air despite my rapid breathing.

I can't fight. I can't move. I have no threats or incentives to offer him. All I can do is ask him. "Please... I don't want to die."

He doesn't move, continuing to drain me. This is cruel. He could've drunk from any of the bodies on the ground. It's like he chose me because he knew that I would feel it – I would experience the dreadful hopelessness that comes with feeling my body shut down.

He finally pulls away, bringing another twinge of pain. His white teeth are colored red with blood – my blood.

I'm in a daze. A warm trickle runs down my chest again. I'm bleeding and unable to reach up to stop it.

He rests his hand on my collar and pinches the skin right next to the wound. I wince.

He keeps his hand steady, and it feels like I'm going numb. I don't know how bad I'm bleeding. I can't even see the cut.

Chapter 2: Marched

After a few minutes, he returns to his dead horse. I'm still tied up, but I'm grateful to have him off me.

He cuts the saddle bag off the horse's harness and tosses it by my feet as if expecting something.

I glance up at him before returning my eyes to the bag. What does he expect me to do? Pick it up? I'm tied to a trunk.

He moves behind the tree. I try twist to get a view of what he's doing, but my binds are so tight that I can hardly move. His fingers brush mine, sending a cold shiver up my arm.

He unties the rope, freeing my wrists. My arms fall to my sides, and I roll the knots out of my sore shoulders. I take a step forward, but my strained legs buckle beneath me, and my knees hit the dirt.

The rope is still attached to my right wrist, but I'm just relieved to be able to move my arms again. I rub my left shoulder, massaging it. My eyes remain down, as if avoiding him will somehow encourage him to do the same for me. This is the first time that he has given me a chance to recover, and I'm going to savor it.

Snatching my wrists up in a tight grip, he yanks both my arms back, making me squeal. By the time I realize what's going on, my wrists are tied behind my back, and he's lifting me to my feet.

He loops the rope around my stomach. My eyes struggle to keep track of his hands in my dazed state. Fear keeps me still. My body is completely at his mercy, and my only security is the hope that he won't hurt me when I'm not trying to fight him.

He yanks on the rope, compressing my middle and making me yelp. Soon the cord is secured with a knot, making it uncomfortably tight. I want to loosen it, but it's by my belly button and my arms are bound behind my back.

He removes his hands, and I immediately lose my balance, tipping forward. I can't use my arms to break my fall!

Before I hit the ground, I'm choked back by my shirt collar. He's holding me up by the back of my shirt. He pulls me upright but keeps his hands around me this time, balancing me like a broom. Draining my blood and binding me has rendered my body so helpless that I can't even stop myself from falling over, but instead of releasing me, he's content with balancing me upright. This is his desired outcome. He wants to keep me completely powerless and at his mercy.

Once I'm steady, he kneels to pick up the eyeball flask. His head is by my waistline. For the first time since he ripped the blanket off me, it feels like I may have an opportunity to beat him. I can knee him in the nose and make a run for it. My heart races as I try to build up the courage. He's digging in the bag that he cut off the horse, oblivious to my impending attack.

I move one foot back to ready my strike, but immediately regret it when I almost lose my balance again. His gaze lands on my fumbling feet. I can't do this. How could I possibly hope to outrun him when I can barely stand? I would make it no more than a few paces before tripping, then I would have to endure his wrath again. He was so oppressive before, handling me as if I had the endurance of ten men and barely allowing me to breathe. What would I have to endure if

I had the audacity to knee him in the nose before failing to escape from his clutches?

He lifts up the bag, pleased with his work. Two leather strips now extrude off the top. He circles me, like a predator. I turn my body to face him, but a heavy hand lands on my shoulder to keep me in place. He rests the bag against my back and threads the straps over my shoulders and under my arms. He's turned it into a backpack and made me into his mule. Lovely.

He picks up the end of the rope connected to my middle and holds it a few inches from my face. "Walk, or you shall be dragged."

I gulp and nod. I suppose that I should just be glad that he has a use for me. As long as he needs someone to carry his stuff, I will be allowed to live.

He walks, and I quickly follow. The short rope leads from his hand to my middle. If it pulls taught, he'll pull me off my feet, and I'll hit the ground face-first with no arms to break my fall.

The long grass and uneven mounds of dirt make walking a challenge. I did not realize how much I used my arms for balance until they were taken away from me.

My gaze lingers on the man leading me forward. His figure forms a dark silhouette which blends in with the night sky. His black cape hangs over his broad shoulders, and it covers him down to his boots. He has the physique of a soldier, but where's his battalion? There were hundreds of them when they burned our village.

I glance back at the barn. The last of my possessions are being left behind, and it makes my heart ache. My coat, the scarf I knitted and the carved dragon hairbrush my brother made for me. They're worthless items to anyone who stumbles across them, but they mean a lot to me. They were the few things I had left from my old life.

* * * * * * *

We've been walking for hours, and the sun is peeking over the horizon. He's taking me north. This is bad. I was fleeing south, to Faria. My brother, Jacob, is expecting me in Fekby, a small village just over the border. Other than a distant uncle I never see, Jacob's the only real family I've got left.

We lived in a small house that our parents left us, and now that it's destroyed, I have to reunite with him in someplace still under human control. He was lucky enough to be traveling when the vampires sacked our village. Before he left on his trading journey, he said I must flee to Fekby if our village was lost. There we will rebuild our lives and put this terrible chapter behind us. But now I'm being dragged north against my will, back to a region infested with vampires. This is a death sentence.

Why is this vampire taking me with him? With his immense strength, he's more than capable of carrying his own bags, and if he didn't hunt us down in the first place, then he'd still have his horse. My little village has done nothing to him or his people. He murdered the men I was traveling with for no reason. We were fleeing from the vampire army, leaving our homes and all our possessions behind to escape them. What could be less threatening than three stonemasons and a farmer running for their lives? He backed us into a corner, forcing the men to make a last-ditch attempt to protect themselves. We had nothing of value. He could've left us alone. With his fast horse, he could have ridden right past us, but he attacked knowing that we couldn't defend ourselves.

"Those men you killed were just stonemasons, running from a village your army burned," I spit.

His gait doesn't waver, and his eyes remain forward. Silence.

I know he can hear me. "Why did you kill them? For sport?"

"Perhaps," he says without looking at me.

His gruff voice sucks the confidence right out of me, reminding me of how he toyed with me when I was tied to the tree, but my anger quickly returns. Killing for sport. "You're a murderer," I growl.

He doesn't even flinch, like my words are meaningless.

"You're a sick cold-blooded monster!" I shout, making sure that he heard every single syllable.

He whips around, and the glare from his red eyes reignites the fear I felt in the barn. I backpedal away, but his hand locks around my shoulder with an iron grip. I shut my eyes and tuck my head down in fear of being struck. Just pinching my shirt would be enough to hold my wobbly frame in place, but his hand rests on my shoulder with the weight of a stone, reminding me how easily he could crush me.

He pulls my hair, and the sudden burn on my scalp makes me wail. My cries are cut short as a piece of fabric is shoved into my mouth. "Nn-" I try protest, but it comes out muffled.

He ties the gag around my head. It digs into my cheeks, forcing them back like a smile, but laughter is the furthest thing from my mind right now.

I shout at him to take it off, but it comes out as mumbling.

He smirks. I want to tear his face off. I shout into the gag again, cursing him and demanding that he removes this degrading accessory, but my words are incomprehensible.

The rope pulls taut, forcing me to follow behind him again.

I let out muffled shouts and coughs. He ignores me, but I don't give up. He burned my home, murdered my companions, took my blood, bound my arms, tied a leash around my midriff and now forced a gag in my mouth. I keep trying to get my words out, to let him know how much I hate him.

After an hour my throat is begging for water. I was thirsty back in the barn, and walking all night and having my blood drained didn't help. I change my tone and ask for water, but it comes out as an unintelligible mumble. Maybe one word would be easier to understand. I try pronouncing 'water' slowly, "Ho-ha."

Nothing.

I could bump into him to get his attention? No, I get the feeling that he wouldn't hold back if he interpreted it as a malicious attack, and I don't have the confidence to move ahead and block his path.

We march on, and soon the sun is high in the sky. My mind plays back silly fantasies in my head, like a squad of the king's knights surrounding us on horses and freeing me from the vampire. They'd release me from my bindings, share their water with me, and carry me home on the back of a horse. Just the thought of sitting down and having something to drink sounds like heaven, but I know that it'll never be anything but a fantasy. If there were any squads of knights left, this vampire would've been hunting them instead of us.

As time passes, my imagined fantasies grow desperate – just involving us accidentally wandering into a marsh, then I could collapse and have some water.

Scanning the horizon, my eyes linger on a wavy pond in the distance – a lake. We could make it there in under an hour if we took a small detour. "Ho-ha!" I gesture my head towards the lake, but he doesn't look at me, not even acknowledging my presence.

Of course he ignores me. He's not thirsty. He has already had his drink. I hate that I have to ask him to do something as simple as take a sip of water. Why would he incapacitate me, forcing me to rely on him, then choose to keep me away from basic things I need to survive? Does he not know that humans need water? Maybe I could nudge him to get his attention?

I lean forward and gently touch his cape with my head – just enough to get his attention, but not enough to be interpreted as an act of aggression.

He stops, and I take a step back.

He turns to face me. I'm glad that I have his attention, but his red eyes make me shiver. My legs bend a little in an instinctive attempt to make myself smaller to show that I don't mean to fight. "Ho-ha," I say in a small voice, gesturing with my head towards the lake.

He doesn't look at the lake. His eyes stay locked on me, and I take another step back. A rock forms in my stomach as I begin to think that I have made a mistake.

In a flash, he backhands me. The force on my cheek sends me crashing down. I hit the ground with a thud. Pain radiates throughout my body, and I let out a long groan.

The rope goes taut, and I'm yanked across the grass by my aching middle. He's walking again, dragging me behind him. I need to get up.

I curl into a ball, push myself upright with my elbows and jump to my feet, stumbling behind him.

My cheek stings and my body aches. He doesn't care about my thirst. He's going to use me up and kill me when I'm too exhausted to walk anymore. No matter how deep you go, he's nothing but a monster.

* * * * * * *

It's just past midday, and it's becoming harder and harder to keep up. The bag on my back feels heavier, my head aches, my chest hurts, and my throat is on fire.

I force myself to keep putting one foot in front of the other, over and over again. There are no more daydreams about knights coming to rescue me or us crossing through a watery marsh. My mind is in a haze, and my ears are ringing. I know that I'm not doing well, but

I'm absolutely powerless to change anything, so I continue along the path that will bring the least pain – putting one foot in front of the other, following behind my vampire captor.

With each step, I grow more and more lightheaded. My vision can't focus on the ground in front of me. Any fear I had about my fate has dissolved from mental exhaustion. The world is spinning around me, twisting as if I'd twirled in circles like a child. I hit the ground.

I can't get up. I don't even know which way is up. The rope pulls taut, and I groan as my stomach is constricted even tighter. My limp body is pulled along the dirt. I shut my eyes as the blades of grass whip over my face. If I could just ignore the pain from the rope, then I'd be able to rest.

He doesn't relent, continuing to drag me. Maybe he'll realize that it'll be easier to take his bag and leave me here, then I could crawl to water. No. I doubt he'd be so kind.

He stops pulling and turns back to face me. Though I can't make out much more than a shadowy frame, I know that he's going to hit me again. There's no way to avoid it. I curl my legs up to my chest to be a little more protected.

He pulls me up by my hair and forces me into a sitting position. The next thing I know, the sharp end of his curved blade is pressed against my throat.

"Stand, or I shall separate your head from your shoulders."

I try move my legs, but nothing happens. My body is exhausted. It's been pushed far beyond what's reasonable. This isn't fair. I tried my best and put my all in, but everything was stacked against me from the beginning. He's the one who weakened me by taking my blood and tying me up, and now he's going to kill me because I can't keep up with a pace of a trained soldier?

I can't make out his expression with my blurry vision. It hurts to talk, so I don't bother trying to beg through the gag. It wouldn't make a difference anyway. I'm never going to see my brother again. I'm going to die in this godforsaken field, murdered by a monster who knows nothing of mercy and cares for no one but himself. The feeling of hopelessness overwhelms me, but my body doesn't have the energy to cry.

My eyes drift from his blurry face to the reflective sword. It shines in the sunlight. This man is so much bigger than me that he doesn't even need a weapon to end my life. It seems almost ridiculous that he would use it to threaten me. I wonder if the blacksmith who forged it knew that it would be used to cut down someone like me? What will this vampire think when he's standing over my dead body – good riddance perhaps? He's so hostile towards me, as if I'm a bane on his life when in reality it is the other way around.

The pressure from the blade disappears, and I'm hoisted up into the air. My world flips upside down. He's carrying me over his shoulder like a sack of potatoes. I lie limp, with no energy to struggle.

* * * * * * *

It's dark by the time he finally puts me down. I've been drifting in and out of consciousness for what feels like hours. He rests my body against the tree and pulls the gag out of my dry mouth.

He shoves a jug against my lips and starts pouring. I gulp the water down, but a good portion of it runs down my shirt. I don't care. It feels like I'm coming back from the dead.

It takes me a moment to notice the lake just a few feet away.

He refills the jug and pours more water in my mouth. I gladly accept it, but he continues for too long, and soon I'm desperate for air and start to choke.

"Drink, human," he growls.

"I'm-I'm trying."

I finish the jug, and he turns to fetch more.

"I've had enough," I say.

He packs it away and then disappears behind the trees. Soon the leaves crunching under his boots is too faint to hear. He's leaving me here, unguarded? I wiggle against my bounds, still tight, but there's nothing stopping me from walking- no, running?

I listen for a few more minutes to make sure he's gone. He left his backpack here, so he's definitely coming back. I rise to my feet and hurry in the opposite direction from where he went. The rope around my middle tightens, and I'm flung back against the ground.

He tethered me. I follow the rope with my eyes from my position on my back. It leads to a branch too high for me to reach with my tied hands. He's subdued me like a mother hiding cookies on a high shelf.

A twig cracks behind me, and I shoot upright.

It's the vampire, carrying a stack of branches. He drops them in a small pit, grabs a flint stone from his backpack and lights the fire.

He falls back on his butt and lets out a sigh. I watch cautiously from my position by the tree. He collected wood and built a fire for the night, then sat down like he's glad to be able to relax at the end of a long day. A human in his position would have done the exact same thing. It's odd seeing him act so normal.

He warms his hands over the fire. The cold night air creeps up my back, and I can't help but be envious.

His gaze lands on me, and I drop my eyes to the fire. The last thing I want is to attract his vicious attention.

"You may approach," he says. "I do not bite... well, at least not twice in one day."

I glare daggers at him. Does he think it's funny that he tied me up and drained my blood?

He doesn't seem to notice or care. He reaches into his bag and pulls out a small leather pouch. I can't quite make out what's inside. He lifts a small brown roll out of the pouch and takes a bite. Food!

Forgetting my previous skepticism, I hurry to the fire and sit opposite him, as far as the rope will let me go. He takes another bite of the dried meat, and my mouth waters. Will he share with me? I mean... he has to? It's not like I can find my own food like this.

He takes another bite, and another, and soon there's not much left. He'll eat it all without a second thought.

"Um..." I interrupt.

His eyes land on me, and he takes another bite, leaving even less.

"Can... can I have some? Please?"

He licks his lips. "It is human."

Chapter 3: Singing for Mercy

My mouth falls open and my face goes pale. The man who's captured me is eating human meat?

His serious expression breaks into a laugh, and he almost falls back in the sand.

After recovering from his moment of joy, he eats the last piece, leaving the pouch empty.

I force a small smile and avert my eyes. It's a joke. He's just messing with me, conjuring up a fun excuse to not have to share the food. I'm sure he derived great joy seeing the look of terror on my face, as if he hasn't scared me enough already. I should've known that it was a trick. He's an asshole.

He retrieves a large leather cylinder from his bag and unrolls it on the sand. It's a sleeping pouch. He climbs inside and turns his back to me.

I stretch out my feet, but the fire is too far away. If I could reach a lit branch, it could burn through my tether.

There's no way out, at least not yet. I should save my energy and get some rest.

I nudge the sand around with my legs to make a little furrow that hugs me on either side.

Minutes pass, but sleep evades me despite my exhaustion. It's not very comfortable. I can't even use my arm as a pillow, and my skin stings wherever it's in contact with the rope.

"Please untie me... so I can sleep," I ask.

He remains still.

I push myself up. "The ropes are tight, and I'll be too tired to walk if I can't rest."

"They prohibit you from slipping away," he says without turning his head.

"Maybe just the rope around my waist? It's pinching my middle, and I can't escape if my hands are still tied."

Nothing.

I need to find something to bargain with, but all I've got left are the clothes on my back. My eyes scan the shore for something of value. Hey, my brother enjoys hearing me sing. "I'll sing a song for you in return."

I don't care if it's embarrassing. It'll be worth it to get rid of the aching in my abdomen, and this is all I can offer him. I clear my throat and take a deep breath. "A storm is loosed upon the-"

"Do you wish to be gagged again?" he interrupts.

I shrink back into myself and don't answer, afraid of that wretched cloth being shoved back in my mouth.

I curl my legs up to my chest and rest my head on my knees. There's a small beetle walking across the mound of sand. The fire reflects off it's shiny shell, making it sparkle. It crests the mound and wanders towards the lake. Soon it's out of my reach. Even that little creature has more freedom than me. It's silly to be envious of a bug, but it takes my mind off my aching stomach.

The vampire rises to his feet, and I nudge away. He towers over me. Did I do something wrong? I was sitting still?

He reaches out, and I shut my eyes and tuck in my head. He pushes my knees down and fidgets with the knot. The rope around my waist falls away. It feels just as uncomfortable coming off as it did going on, but relief follows right after.

"No more whining," he says.

I nod, and he returns to his pouch.

I maneuver my tied hands to nudge up the hem of the shirt. There's a red rope pattern imprinted across my stomach and over my belly button, but at least there's no bruising.

The rope around my wrists is still tethered to the tree branch, so I lay down again and try to make myself comfortable. The fire helps, but the cold air still nips at my exposed skin. All I've got is a pair of long pants, a short-sleeve shirt and cheap leather shoes. My coat was left back at the barn.

The vampires head rests on white fluffy wool. The whole sleeping pouch must be lined with it. It looks warm and cozy. I shut my eyes and pretend I'm somewhere else - camping with my brother, Jacob.

* * * * * * *

I watch the sunrise from my nook in the sand. It's already morning, and I barely got any sleep thanks to the cold.

A splash of freezing water hits my skin. I squeal and jump upright. The vampire has an empty jug in his hand.

"I was awake," I spit.

"And now you're energized. Get up. We depart soon."

He packs away the jug and rolls up his sleeping pouch.

I need to pee. It takes a minute to get on my feet with stiff muscles and tied hands. This wretched rope leashes me so I'm never more than a few yards from the tree, which is right in his line of sight.

"Untie me. I need to pee."

"I don't see how those two are related, human."

"My name's not human, it's Julia, and I need privacy."

"Then I'm afraid you'll find the rest of this journey rather uncomfortable."

I shoot him a dirty look, but he's too busy fiddling with his alchemy potions to notice.

I can't hold it much longer, and asking him to stop traveling later would be even more embarrassing. He seems rather preoccupied with whatever he's fiddling with in his bag, so I take the opportunity and scurry behind the tree. I retie my belt at the back where it's easier to reach.

My head pokes around the trunk. He's waiting on the shore.

"Sit," he orders, patting the sand between his legs.

I gulp. "I'm happy here."

"Do not force my hand."

I don't want to be that close to him. Weighing my options in my head, the look on his face says he's not kidding, and I'm still leashed. I have to listen, fighting him here will just get me hurt.

I cautiously approach, not taking my eyes off him, and take a seat between his feet, as far from him as possible while still appearing as if I'm obeying his instructions.

He leans forward, pressing his torso against my bound arms. His hands creep around my middle, and I stiffen.

"What are you doing?" I blurt out.

His big arms wrap around my chest, and their weight rests on my small frame.

"No, no, no. I haven't done anything wrong," I cry, shaking. His arms are like stone. I'm tied up, I'm trapped, and I don't know what's happening.

He blows my hair off my shoulder and sniffs my skin. My heart falls into my stomach. I open my mouth to protest, but before I get a word out, his teeth sink into my flesh.

I shriek from the pain. It's like a blade is being wedged into my neck. I try push away from him, but his arms don't let me move an inch.

"Please stop, please." I can't take this again.

He keeps drinking, and I can feel the blood flowing from my body. My breathing quickens, and my heart beats like I've run a mile.

"Please." I hate this. I hate that I'm so weak that he can draw the life from my body as he pleases.

It takes a good few minutes before he's had his fill. He removes his teeth and pinches the skin near the bite. I sit still, feeling defeated.

He fetches a jug of water from the lake and presses it to my lips. I open my mouth, but his impatient pouring leads to half of it going down my shirt.

He removes the rope from the tree and ties it around my waist like before. It's still tight, but not as bad.

The bag is secured to my back, then his hands shoot under my arms and yank me upright.

"You don't have to be so rough," I grumble.

"I'll consider your suggestion." He jerks the rope, almost causing me to lose my balance.

* * * * * * *

I didn't walk like this when fleeing with Neil and his companions. We'd take breaks, search for fruit and hunt animals, whereas the man ahead of me marches on and on, unrelenting.

Just thinking about food makes my stomach rumble. My gaze lands back on him. He doesn't look the slightest bit tired. He really isn't human.

I hurry up to walk alongside him. "What's your name?" I ask.

He doesn't spare me a glance.

"I told you mine – it's Julia. Aren't you going to tell me yours?"

"You may address me as Master," he says.

"I am no slave."

"And I suppose the rope binding your wrists is the latest fashion?"

"I may be your captive, but I am not your slave," I spit.

"Relax, human. I won't be needing a slave for very much longer."

I perk up. "You're going to let me go?"

He keeps his eyes forward.

"When will-"

"I gather that you weren't known among your crummy village for your intellect."

My heart sinks. He's going to auction me off? Or worse – kill me? Why would he do such a thing instead of just letting me go? I won't see him again either way, but he could take my life just for his own entertainment.

"Does tearing others down help you feel better about your moral shortcomings?" I grumble.

"You know nothing about me, human."

"And you know nothing about me either. You dismiss me and my home without taking a minute to understand it."

"If your home was so great, then why were you sleeping in a barn?" he mocks.

"Because of monsters like you."

He grabs my chin and forces my head up.

"Mind your tongue, human." His hand is so tight it makes my jaw ache. "There will not be another warning."

I quickly nod the best I can under his grip, and he shoves my head away. I need to escape – soon.

An hour passes without us saying a word to one another. That suits him fine. He knows where we're going, and I'm the one lacking in information. It couldn't hurt to ask a harmless question, right? He only seems to mind when I call him out. I take a deep breath and build up my courage.

"Where are we going?"

"North," he grunts.

I can see the sun too. "Anywhere north in particular?"

"That is not of your concern."

Dead end. Maybe I should lead in with a more casual question? I rack my mind trying to think of what to ask. He's a vampire, and I've never spoken to one before. This week was the first time I even laid eyes on one of them, and that was from a long distance, though I do wish I could've remained ignorant.

I settle on a question I've had since I was a child. "Is it true that vampires don't like garlic?"

"Why would we eat a plant?" he says as if I'm a fool.

"You don't eat any?"

"No. Do humans?" He points at the ground. "Does that grass look appetizing to you?"

I ignore his question figuring that he's just making fun of me. "Then what do you eat?"

"Do you believe I bit you this morning for my own amusement?" He glances back at me with a smirk, and I shudder. I twist my neck trying to get a glimpse of the bite mark, but it's to no avail. That puts a sharp end to our conversation, killing my initial enthusiasm.

The sun is setting, and we're heading straight for an oak forest.

"It's almost dark. Aren't we going to set up camp?" I ask. I'm also thirsty, and the water skin in the bag on my back has been taunting me for the last hour.

"No," he says.

"We can't go through the forest at night. The scarlet wolves will make a meal of us."

"Right." He doesn't slow down.

"I'm serious. I've lived here my whole life. They're not like normal wolves. They're vicious. You can't scare them off, and standing your ground doesn't help."

We pass through the tree line, and I pull against him, angling myself against the rope to make as much resistance as possible. "You're going to get us killed!"

He wraps the rope around his hand and gives it a hard tug. I'm jerked off my feet and land on my side.

I let out a groan from the impact. He keeps pulling, dragging me deeper into the forest.

Chapter 4: Thrown to the Wolves

I wiggle around and stumble back to my feet. "I'm telling you the truth. We'll be eaten alive."

He's not listening. Soon we're so deep in the forest that the grass planes are out of sight. A shiver runs down my spine. I've just got to hope that I'm wrong. My pace quickens so that there's barely a gap between us. It would be better to be at his mercy than in the jaws of a wolf.

The last rays of sunset disappear, making it near impossible to see. I keep my eyes open, scanning the thick bush surrounding us. The hairs on the back of my neck stand straight. If the wolves find us, I'm done for. My hands are tied, and the bag on my back doesn't help.

Maybe that's his plan? If things go south, he can just outrun me, and I'll be sacrificed as a distraction.

I wiggle against my bounds, but they don't budge. I don't have any options. I've just got to hope that we get lucky.

We walk for an hour, and the trees open up a bit. A forest fire went through this area, clearing the underbrush. It's eerily quiet, with the only sound coming from leaves crunching beneath our feet. No crickets, no birds, no bugs.

The vampire freezes, and my stomach does a flip. I peek around his cape. The sight makes me want to scream, but I hold it in.

Two eyes, glowing in the moonlight, and teeth tinted red with blood. It's a scarlet wolf. Their mouths are always bleeding, like they have some disease.

It lets out a growl, and I hold back a whimper. The last thing I need right now is to sound like a small animal.

The vampire reaches for his weapon. Another growl comes from behind, and I nearly jump out of my skin. I whip around to see two, no three, no four pairs of eyes. They're almost as tall as me, but they stand on four legs.

"They're everywhere," I whisper.

He takes a step to the side, and I follow him. He slowly moves to an opening between the pack. I stick to him like glue. I've lost count of how many eyes there are.

In a flash, he leaps up a tree, leaving me alone on the ground. The wolves charge, triggered by his sudden movement. A sea of grey and red is about to engulf me.

My hands are tied. I can't climb. "Help me! Help me! Help me!"

The rope tightens around my middle, and I'm yanked up into the air.

He places me on the branch with him. It takes me a second to catch my breath. A loud bark from below makes me yelp. He chuckles and unties the bag from my back. "Scared?"

I ignore his taunt. My eyes linger on the mess of fangs and claws below. My heart is hammering against my chest, and the adrenaline has me shaking. I can't balance on the branch with my tied arms, so he keeps me steady with a hand on my shoulder.

I fall.

The very hand that was supposed to keep me up, pushes me off. All the muscles in my core tense, like I'm about to break in two. The air rushes over my skin, taking the beads of sweat. I catch a glimpse of him as my body plummets down. He's grinning.

I come to a hard stop just a few feet above their snapping teeth. The rope around my waist is the only thing keeping me from certain death. He's dangling me over them.

I fold my legs into my chest to try keep away from their sharp teeth. He doesn't need me anymore. He's going to feed me to them. I'm going to die like an animal.

The rope slips further. He's lowering me inch by inch, bringing me closer and closer to death. The wolves' bleeding gums color their teeth red. Their deafening barking and endless growling overwhelm my ears, and their putrid breath and sweaty coats assault my nose.

They jump for me, their teeth snapping only inches from my skin. I curl into myself, shut out the world and think back to just a week ago, before the vampires came. The farm, my home, and my friends. I miss them dearly. Their lives were cut short, and now it's my turn. I remember laughing with Jacob, when I was so happy. Jacob- Tears rolls down my cheeks. He'll never know what happened to me. How long will he wait before realizing I'm dead?

My body is lowered further. My muscles tense for the imminent pain, and I imagine myself being torn to pieces.

The rope is yanked in the opposite direction, knocking the air out of my lungs and making me cough, and I'm pulled back up onto the branch.

The vampire's hand rests on my shoulder to keep me balanced. He's laughing. "You are easily fooled, human."

The wolves growl and scratch at the base of the tree. I turn to hide my face. I can't stop crying, and my whole body is shaking.

He goes quiet, and soon the only sound is the wolves snarling and my own sobbing.

"It was only a gag," he says.

So playing with my life is a joke. Is that supposed to make me feel better?

He touches my hair, and I flinch.

He pulls me close, leaning my side against his chest, then wraps his arms around me. I'm trembling, and he can feel it too.

"I will not let the beasts take you," he says. Empty words.

* * * * * * *

My eyes peek open. On instinct, I try wipe away the sleep before the rope pulls my hands back.

I jerk upright at the realization that my head is leaning against the vampire's chest. His arm is still around my small frame, preventing me from tipping over.

I look up at him. There are bags under his eyes. He must've been too worried about falling to sleep.

"Morning," I squeak.

He looks down at me with those red eyes, and I shrink into myself. "It is," he yawns.

His hands creep under my arms, making my body stiffen. He lowers me to the ground, letting me fall the last few feet, then jumps down himself with a heavy thud.

I try face him, but a hand around my arm keeps me in place. My shoulders arch up, shielding my neck. Having him behind me puts my nerves even more on edge.

To my surprise, he releases my wrists. The rope peels away from my raw skin, making me wince. It's been stuck there for over two days.

I finally get a look at my wrists. They've been impressed with the rope pattern and are scabbed and bleeding along the edges.

"Remove your tunic," he orders.

"What?" I clutch my shirt collar. "I won't undress for you."

"You will do as I say, slave. Remove it."

I take a step back. "No."

There's a flash of anger in his eye.

In one quick movement, I'm shoved to the ground, and he's straddling me. His fingers lock around the hem of my shirt and yank it up.

"No!" I grab the material and pull it back down.

The next thing I know, both my hands are pinned above me, and he pulls the shirt up and over my head, leaving only my linen bra to offer any form of modesty.

To my surprise, the weight on my legs disappears. "That attitude will get you killed," he says with my shirt in hand. He draws his curved sword and starts cutting. "You seem too dim to recognize the situation you find yourself in."

My heart aches as one of the last of my possessions is destroyed. Is this some kind of punishment?

He cuts it further, then lays it out on a rock. He rinses it with the water from the skins, then pours some sort of elixir over the material. It has a strong scent of smoke and salt.

"Making another gag?" I grumble, "You're morally abhorrent, so you want to silence me before I call you out again?"

He marches towards me, grabs my arm and wraps the material around my wrist. He finishes the bandage with a knot, yanking it tight and making me wince. "Don't tempt me."

He repeats the process with my other wrist, then tosses the remains of my shirt back to me.

I run it through my fingers. It seems mostly intact. I pull it over myself, only to discover it's become a lot shorter. My middle is bare.

He guides my arms behind my back, and my heart sinks. I was hoping he wouldn't tie me up again. He binds my wrists with the same rope, but it's looser this time. I resist the urge to wiggle my arms to test the restraints while under his gaze.

His arms wrap around my torso, and I can feel his warm breath on the back of my neck. I brace myself for what's coming. At least I'll get water afterwards.

A whimper escapes me as his fangs pierce my skin. He punctures the same spot every time.

My heart rate increases to accommodate for the lost blood. At least I know it'll be over soon.

He removes his razor teeth and pinches my skin to let the wound seal.

I'm allowed to drink from the water skin, and we continue our trek.

* * * * * * *

The lack of food is starting to take its toll. I'm already tired, and we've only just begun walking. I've figured out that he's only dragging me along with him to have his daily blood meals. He wouldn't need me if his horse wasn't killed. Which wouldn't have happened if he didn't hunt us down, and we wouldn't have been fleeing if those vampires didn't torch our village.

Uncle Ivan is a member of the Huntsmen, a brave group of heroes who pledge to protect humans from vampires. Though I don't know him well, Jacob often visits him on his travels. I had hoped that the Huntsmen would defend our homes, but they must've been spread too thin. There was no one to help us when these demons came.

"Why did you burn my village?" I spit.

"You would not understand, human," he dismisses me.

"It's Julia, and I'm more capable than you give me credit. If you were trying to send a message to the king, then why not burn his palace instead of my home?"

"Your king is dead."

King Howard is dead? I didn't realize that our country's situation was so dire.

"If the king is dead, then why burn my village? There was no gold or silver."

"We have no need for vacant straw huts."

"They weren't empty. I was a resident, and I was just lucky enough to get away... at least at first," I mumble the last part under my breath.

"I already warned that you would not understand. 'Tis as frivolous as explaining to a bird why its tree was logged."

It's not that I can't understand, it's that he can't be bothered to tell me.

He reaches out his hand, and I tense. "Don't worry your little human mind with what has happened or what will happen," he says, rubbing my head. "Just do as I instruct."

"I am not a child," I spit.

We walk further, and I spot something red in the corner of my eye. An Apple! We're under an apple tree!

"Look! Apples!" I'm practically dancing for joy.

"Fascinating," he says without slowing down.

"Can we take a short break? I'm hungry."

He doesn't stop.

I dig my feet into the ground and pull against the rope, but he overpowers me with little effort. I'm not going to let this opportunity pass by. Moving beside him, I position a tree trunk between us and make a quick circle around it, as much as the short rope will allow. Now there's a knot. Overpower that, asshole.

He yanks on the rope, but the tree doesn't budge. He raises his hand to strike me. I shut my eyes and tuck my head into my shoulder. "Please don't. I just want to eat."

Nothing happens.

I look back at the apples, and he follows my gaze.

"You eat that?" he asks.

A wave of relief washes over me, and I relax my shoulders. "Yea, we eat fruit, nuts, berries, grain and meat."

"So you are like monkeys."

I don't appreciate the comparison, but I keep my mouth shut for the sake of getting the apple.

"Untangle yourself from the tree," he instructs.

I do as he says, and my face lights up when he begins picking apples.

He carries back five big juicy ones, and my mouth is watering. He holds one up for me to bite, but I hold myself back. There's something off about it. It's discolored, covered in little holes and doesn't smell right.

"Can you open it?" I ask.

He breaks it in half, and I jerk away in disgust. It's rotten, infested with tiny bugs. I scan the other apples. They've all got the same holes.

"Never mind," I mumble, trying to internally reassure myself that real food will come soon.

When I look up again, he's gone, and my rope is tied to a branch.

"Mr Vampire?" I call.

A few minutes pass before his footsteps return. He steps out the bushes, and I can't believe the sight in front of me. He's carrying at least twenty apples in his cape, and they're fresh!

He breaks one in half and holds it up for me to eat.

I take a huge bite. The sweet and smooth texture makes me groan. I take another and another, barely chewing before swallowing. It's a relief to have something in my stomach again.

He moves his fingers around the apple, giving me a new spot to bite. I was so hungry that it only now crosses my mind that I'm eating out of his hand. I'm a little embarrassed eating like his pet, but it's either that or starve, and I don't think he'll be so cruel as to strike my face while I'm leaning in.

Soon the apple is finished, and I look at him with pleading eyes.

He breaks another one in half and lets me eat. It takes another four apples before I'm full.

He packs the rest in the bag on my back, and I crane my neck to try get a view. There's food for days.

* * * * * * * *

We set up camp at sunset, which involves him foraging for branches, starting a fire, removing my backpack and laying out his sleeping pouch, all while I just stand there with my arms tied.

He lets me drink from the water skin, then anchors the end of my rope to a tree.

He munches down on the same dried meat over the fire. Wiggling my hands confirms my suspicions from this morning. My bounds aren't as tight, probably to allow my wounds to heal. I could stretch my arms under myself if the rope wasn't also wrapped around my middle. If he takes it off for me to sleep, I may be able to slip away.

"Can you untie the rope from my waist? My tied wrists will still prevent me from escaping."

He moves in, standing uncomfortably close. I step back, but he pinches a lock of my hair, not rough enough to hurt, but enough to hold me in place. "Escape is on your mind?" he says, his hand just inches from my face.

My stomach curls up. "N-no," I stutter, "I just- I just- You said last time-"

"Need I explain the punishment for trying to flee?"

My gaze falls to his feet. "I just want it off so I can sleep."

"You didn't protest about it last night."

"I was afraid that you'd throw me to the wolves." It's half true. I was in such a state that I wasn't paying attention to my body's discomfort.

He finally moves his hand away from my face, and I let out a sigh of relief. He unties the waist rope and returns to the fire.

I sit opposite him to avoid arousing suspicion. I lay down, facing away as to not give away anything with my expression. As soon as he's asleep, I'll make my move.

Chapter 5: Escape

An hour passes, and my insides are bubbling. I turn to face him, careful not to make a sound.

The back of his head is only just visible from his pouch. Is he asleep yet? Should I whisper to check? No. Don't chance it.

The fire dies down, and the cold night air creeps in. My stomach is doing backflips. He kills humans for sport. I don't want to imagine what he'd do to a prisoner caught escaping.

The minutes tick by. I have to do something. If I keep wasting time, it'll be morning, and we'll continue traveling. If we reach a vampire city, he won't need me anymore. He'll kill me just like the others. Tomorrow night may be too late. I have to do this, and I have to do it now.

I curl up my knees to my chest and force my bound hands under my butt. My torso squeezes as small as possible as my hands push further and further. The rope is looser than before, and the bandages protect my cut wrists from the pressure.

Air is forced out of my lungs as my hands push over the last few inches. I suck in a deep breath the second they're passed the threshold. I thread each leg under my arms and bring my hands up to my face. There's no going back now.

Maneuvering myself is trivial now that my arms are in front. I bite and pull at the rope binding my wrists, coating my tongue with the taste of dry grass. The adrenaline is making me shake.

Finally, the rope loosens, and I shake it off my bandaged wrists.

There's nothing hindering me now. I just need to sneak away. I take off my shoes and carry them. Going bare foot will be quieter. My bare feet will feel for twigs and dry leaves, making sure it's safe to take a step.

I rise to my feet and scan the horizon. We're in an open field with a few scattered trees. He'll be able to see me a mile away. Was this a mistake? My eyes land back on the rope, then on his sleeping figure. It's impossible to retie my own wrists. The only way is forward.

I take a step, toe first to check for any twigs in the long grass, then another, and another. Step after step. I don't look back.

My pace quickens as I get into the rhythm. Soon I'm far enough away to safely put on my shoes. I slip them on my feet and start running.

"Human!" There's a blood-chilling screech behind me, and my face goes pale.

Run. I don't look back. My legs move as fast as they can carry me. The cold night air rushes over my skin like a gale-force wind.

My lungs are burning. My overworked legs struggle not to slip on the dirt. Footsteps are gaining on me.

I'm struck on the head and go tumbling to the ground. The dirt and grit scrape up my arms, and a searing pain radiates through my skull.

I push myself up onto all fours, but a hard boot kicks me in the side, sending me back down. I scream as the iron-toed boot hits my abdomen a second time. My body curls inwards to protect my vulnerable stomach, but it does little to stop his onslaught.

"You swine!" he shouts over me.

I cry out again as he kicks my middle. The burning pain makes me wail. My fingers claw at the dirt to try drag myself away. Stop! Stop! Stop! Another kick in the same spot, making the burning even worse. "Pea-" I try beg but my mouth can't form words. It's like a knife is twisting inside me. My muscles stress and kick and flail to make it stop. He kicks again, and fire runs from the impact to my core.

He finally relents, but the pain lingers. I can't breathe.

"You expected to flee!?" His eyes burn with hate.

I shut my eyes and suck in a breath despite my burning diaphragm. My arms are yanked above my head, making my aching muscles scream. No more. Please no more.

My whole body is pulled upright by the arms. Every movement brings a new wave of agony. My vision is blurry from tears. Dirt covers my stinging arms, and my back fights to stay curled to minimize the burning in my middle.

I'm placed on his lap, and my body cries out from the movement. His arms snake around my bruising torso. His heavy breath pours over the back of my neck. Iron arms compress my middle, making me scream again. He relieves the pressure, and my screaming turns to sobbing.

My back is pressed against his stone chest. I try push away, but he grabs both my arms and holds them down.

No more. No more. He has to stop. I struggle against him, but he compresses my hands in his, and I cry out again. It's like they're being crushed between stones. My body curls into itself, and he releases the pressure after my tearful surrender.

His thumbs creep up the back of my hand, and his fingers clamp around mine.

"These fingers," he whispers into my ear, making my blood run cold, "they are mischievous, removing your bounds."

My breath sticks in my throat.

"They have no use to me, just a nuisance really."

My heart drops into my stomach. He puts his thumbs at the base of my fingers and pushes my digits backwards.

The pain runs up my arms and into my core, and I let out a terrible cry. They're right on the edge. If he pushes any further, they'll break. I cry and wail from both the pain and the reality of losing my hands.

He stops pushing and lets my fingers sit straight again. The pain disappears, but he keeps his grip on them.

I'm sobbing aloud. Everything hurts, and he's going to break my hands. The world is obscured by tears. I don't move a muscle, sitting as still as I can other than my uncontrollable trembling.

I'm at his mercy, and he wants me to suffer. I don't know what to do. My voice can only stutter, unable to string words together. His hands stay locked around mine. I don't resist. I don't push against him in anyway, terrified to anger him further.

Tears fall on my hands and his. He's silent, and the night is quiet except for my sobbing. We're alone here. There's not a soul for miles - no one to save me.

He caresses my fingers with his thumb, and I let out a whimper. He lets go of my hands, as if it was in response to my fear.

My arms lie limp, paralyzed from shock. He engulfs my small frame.

"Will you flee again?" he whispers from behind.

"No." I shake my head.

He pushes me off him, and I groan from the movement. He rises to his feet and pulls me up by the arm. My legs don't work on the first try, and his hand stays clamped, resting all my weight on my shoulder.

He marches back to the smoldering fire. I force my legs to listen and gain back my footing, relieving the tension on my shoulder.

My muscles can barely push me forward without aggravating the pain in my abdomen. I stumble again and again, but the vampire doesn't slow down, and his rigid grip keeps me upright.

He pushes down on my shoulder once we reach the fire, and I take the hint to sit. Rubbing the dirt off my arms reveals shallows scratches with trace amounts of blood.

He picks up the rope. My neck strains trying to meet his gaze, so I stare at his knees instead.

"How did you free yourself?" he asks.

My arms wrap around my aching stomach. "I-I slipped my hands in front and b-bit the rope," I say, barely above a whisper.

"Are you trying to deceive me?"

"No, no-" I stutter, and another wave a panic follows. I'm not lying, and he's going to beat me further because he doesn't believe me. I feel so utterly powerless. He caught up to me in seconds. His arms are like iron. He's beyond human. I tuck in my head and curl into myself to prepare for the next wave of kicks.

A yelp escapes me as he yanks my arms behind my back and clamps them together with one hand. He ties each wrist to the opposite elbow, giving me absolutely no movement at all.

The rope is extended down and looped around my bare middle. He pulls it tight, pinching my skin, and connects the other end to a high branch.

My arms can't move an inch. They're folded behind my back.

His footsteps return to his side of the smoldering fire. I blink until my vision is clear. Breathing a deep breath makes me wince from the pain. The cut edge of my shirt stops half-way over the spot where he repeatedly kicked me.

Shrugging my shoulders up reveals more of my reddening skin. The pain flares up from any exertion on my diaphragm. It emanates from the spot just below my ribs. That's something to be thankful for, that my bones aren't broken.

My eyes wander back to him. He's back in his sleeping pouch, though is probably still listening.

I'm sitting up, but my tied arms can't provide support to help me down. If my body wasn't in such pain, I'd just let myself fall over.

I lean back, as if I was doing the second half of a sit up, but a sharp pain in my core muscles makes my back shoot up again.

Leaning forward, I let my head hit the ground first, providing a column of support as I lay my aching body sideways. I'm down but have no hope of getting back up in the morning.

My eyes close, and I try get some rest. Hopefully the pain will have subsided tomorrow. I vow that if I'm ever in a position of power, I will never inflict pain for the sake of it.

The cold air creeps in, making me miss the bottom third of my shirt.

* * * * * * *

It's morning, and the vampire has woken up. The combination of cold, pain and tight bonds kept me awake. Though I am feeling better. Just letting my muscles rest did wonders for my soreness, even if they were tied an awkward position. My arms are out of view, but the lack of stinging and slight itching suggests that the scratches are healing.

I'm lying flat against the ground, and the rope makes sitting up impossible. Just lifting my head is more than my neck can bare right now.

"Mr Vampire?" I call with my face against the ground.

"Human?" His eyes are drawn to me. Being so low makes him appear enormous.

"Can you help me up, please?" He may still be ticked off, so I opt to be polite. I'm hoping he'll just get the blood meal over with so I can have water.

He lifts me up, and I cross my legs to avoid falling over. To my surprise, he pulls out an apple. Withholding food as punishment didn't seem like a stretch, but I suppose it's more advantageous to him to have a strong mule.

I keep my eyes on him as I take bites, still unsure.

He makes no sudden moves, looking exactly as he did when feeding me the first time. From his expression, it doesn't appear that he holds any new animosity towards me.

After breakfast, he secures his arms around me and has his drink. It still hurts, but I've learned that staying still makes it easier.

He gives me water, then the bag is secured on my shoulders, and we march again.

The spot on my middle has morphed into a big purple bruise. Anyone looking would know that this vampire is a violent man. Though the aching has gone down enough for me to walk with minimal discomfort. He must've known precisely where to strike to maximize pain without hindering my ability to walk.

My gaze lands back on him.

"We've been walking together for almost four days, but I still don't know your name," I say.

"As I said before, call me Master." He grins.

"I'm serious." I can't imagine how sharing his name could be detrimental to his cause.

"I am Lord Ralan."

"Well, Lord Ralan, I'd shake your hand but-"

"Not Ralan," he interrupts, "Surely you humans are not that dense? Rah-lan."

"It's not from my language, and at least I care to learn your name, something you couldn't be bothered to do for me. You don't have to be so rude."

"You know, Julia, usually slaves try win their master's favor, but you seem intent on losing it."

I stop for a second. He was listening.

We travel the rest of the day in silence. I refrain from asking any more questions. While the bruising on my stomach looks bad, I haven't had trouble keeping food and water down. My body is recovering, and there are no signs of life-threatening complications.

At the end of the day, we stop at the top of a hill, and he removes the bag from my back. The sun is down, and it's cold. I don't expect to get much sleep tonight either.

I spot a small settlement in the distance, and my heart stops. It's less than a day's walk away.

"Is that where we're going?" I blurt out.

"You ask many questions," he sighs.

Sparks fly off the flint as he strikes it over the kindling. I'm pretty sure I already know the answer anyway.

He lays out his sleeping pouch, and I huddle up in a little nook in the rocks. It's freezing.

There's a sinking feeling in my stomach. He slaughtered Neil and his friends without hesitating, and he won't need my blood after we reach the trade post.

"Lord Rahlan," I begin, "can I ask just one question?"

There's a long pause, but he finally answers. "One question."

I take in a breath to keep my voice steady. "When we reach the trade post tomorrow, am I going to die?"

He meets my gaze, not answering immediately, like he's thinking it through.

"No."

Relief washes over me, and I can breathe again. A heavy load has been lifted off my shoulders, but the weight comes back a second later. "Then what are you going to do with me?"

He doesn't look up from the fire. Right - one question.

Did he even tell the truth? Maybe he's just lying to keep me docile. The thought of escaping crosses my mind again, but I quickly swat it away. I've no chance of sneaking away after last night.

I shut my eyes and try focus on pleasant thoughts, like Jacob. I wonder if he's made it to Faria yet? He's an experienced traveler. I bet he's already picked out our new home. It could be a castle. He's always wanted to live in one, ever since we were children.

Chapter 6: Betrayal

A boot on my shoulder shakes me awake. It's morning, and Rahlan's standing over me. The freezing air didn't allow me much rest. I can't get up on my own with my arms tied wrist to elbow, but he's looking at me expectantly.

"Good morning?" I say from my place on the ground.

His rough hands flip me upright and release my wrists. "You have a minute to stretch."

I spread my arms and wave them in a circle around me. It feels great to have them free again. I loosen the rope around my midriff so it's more comfortable.

I reach for an apple in the bag, but he slaps my hand away.

"I just wanted breakfast," I mumble, rubbing my sore hand.

"Times up." He picks up the rope. I shoot up and back away as he steps closer.

"Don't tie me yet. I won't fight. Please."

He grabs my shoulder and yanks me into his stone chest, then spins me around and pulls my arms behind my back. "You do not decide when you are bound."

"That's why I'm asking. Please let me eat first. It makes no difference to you, but it means a lot to me."

His breath tickles the back of my neck as he mulls it over.

He releases my arms, and I stumble forward.

"Don't do anything you'll regret," he warns.

I hug my middle and peer back at the bag. Am I allowed to take from it now?

He answers my question by handing me two apples and the water skin. I waste no time munching them down. It's a welcome change to eating out of his hand.

I gulp down the water, but he yanks it away. "We're far from a river,"
he says.

He prowls behind me and rests his heavy hands on my shoulders,
making me flinch. He leans in takes in a deep breath, and a chill runs
down my spine. He's sniffing his food.

His hands snap to my sides, making me yelp. "Something got you on
edge?" he teases.

"Gee," I begin, "I wonder what it could-"

His fangs pierce my neck, making me cut myself off with a squeak.

He's holding my chest, but this is the first time he's drunk from me
with my arms free. I could fight back, but I know better. It'll net me
nothing but a few minutes of struggling and extra pain.

He finishes his meal and immediately binds my arms again. I was
hoping that my obedience would have earned me some trust, but I
suppose not.

"I know I can be rather intimidating, but are these ropes really necessary?" I ask.

"Think of it like leashing an untrained dog," he says. "'Tis just a pain to have to chase them down." He pulls the rope tight on the final word, making me wince.

"I'm not a dog."

"You're right, it doesn't seem very appropriate. Dogs don't whine as much as you."

The bag is tied to my back, and the rope around my waist forces me to follow. We head straight for the trade post, and the uneasy feeling in my stomach grows. I hope he keeps his word.

* * * * * * * *

We pass through a gap between the log walls that acts as a gate. They protect four wooden houses, a tavern and a stable. I recognize the architecture. This is a human settlement, well it was a human settlement. Now it's crawling with vampires. They're pale, and every one of them is a good head and half taller than me. They're all men – soldiers.

I've never seen so many vampires this close. I stick to Rahlan like glue. A few notice my presence and shoot me dirty looks. More and more start to stare. I'm a sheep being led through a wolves' den. My gaze drops to the boots of the vampire leading me.

He stops, and I keep my gaze down. It feels like every set of eyes is on me, burning a hole in the back of my skull. Why are they acting like I'm an intruder? I'm a prisoner. My bound arms along with the rope leading from my bruised waist to Rahlan's hand should be a pretty strong indicator that I don't want to be here.

Rahlan introduces himself to the vampire manning the stables. He's got black hair with an uneven beard and shares Rahlan's pale skin and blood red eyes.

"Do you have a chart?" Rahlan asks. I nudge closer to him in fear of being snatched away from behind. Better the devil you know than the devil you don't, and I don't know if he'd bother pursuing me if I was snatched by one of these men.

"Here," the stable master knocks his knuckles against a wooden board. I peek around Rahlan to get a view. There's a map carved on the stable wall.

It's covered in words that look completely foreign to me. I'm no scribe, but I can at least recognize the names of the villages near mine, but nothing here is ringing any bells.

"Where are we?" Rahlan asks.

"Here." The stable master pokes a hut symbol on the board.

"This is my heading," Rahlan points to a city. "How many days need I travel?"

There's a dark groove between the hut and the city. Is it a canyon or a river? My eyes dart around the map. It can't be a river, they're painted blue. It's a border. Crud. He's taking me back to his country.

Once we're over that border, there'll be no chance of escape. I won't just be leaving my country, I'll be leaving any hope of freedom too.

"'Tis one day's ride by horse, three by foot," the stable master says.

That's why he didn't kill me. He still needs me. The clock is ticking. I have to get away in the next three days or I'm dead meat. I scan the map from top to bottom. The blue lines are rivers, so the big blue line must be the biggest river – the Gaultane. We'll travel straight from the hut to the city, so we'll pass right over it just before the border.

There's a little castle symbol on the river. I heard stories that Lord Guerin built his castle in the middle of one. It's on our side of the border, so it must be Guerin. If I could make it to the castle, I'll be safe. Rahlan is strong, but he can't siege a castle alone. I'll be free.

"I wish to purchase a horse," Rahlan says. What? If he gets a horse, I'm finished.

"A gold piece or ten silver."

"Five Prymni?" Rahlan offers.

"Prymni will not suffice." The stable master shakes his head. "Maybe the barman will trade you silver for Prymni." He gestures to the tavern on the opposite side, and Rahlan makes his way to the door.

He grabs my bound arm and pulls me inside the dimly lit bar. The air is heavy with tobacco. There are humans in here! There's a truce? Did they make a deal? Can I make one? I scan the room looking for a human in charge, but my enthusiasm evaporates when I realize what's going on.

There's no truce. Human women sit between vampire men, and bite marks litter their skin. They're prisoners like me. They killed the men and kept the women as blood meals.

My stomach twists into a knot when the corner table catches my eye. There are women wearing next to nothing on the vampires' laps. Some kissing the monsters, who have their filthy claws digging into their skin. One is dancing, giving a performance to a smiling bloodsucker.

A poor soul watches me from across the room. She's being fed on, her frail frame entrapped behind huge arms. She's terrified. Her eyes beg me to save her.

Rahlan pushes me towards the bar. His fingers stay locked around my arm.

"Do you trade for silver?" he asks the barman.

I glance at the woman next to me. There are bite marks on her arms and legs, some fresh enough to source a small trickle of blood. She's not particularly well covered either. None of them are. They have their shirts torn to expose their necks, shoulders and arms.

"What have you got?" the barman asks.

Rahlan lets go of my arm, reaches into the bag on my back and drops a handful of glass pieces on the counter. They're gorgeous little tokens, like tiny stained-glass windows. "Ten Prymni," Rahlan says.

"Your king's tokens are worthless here."

The barman's eyes land on me, and I suddenly feel very self-conscious about the state of my clothing. My shirt is torn at my middle, and my arms and neck are completely vulnerable to a set of vampire fangs. I take a step back behind Rahlan.

"You've got a blood bag. You need all of it to yourself?" the barman asks.

I feel sick to my stomach. I've only just started getting use to Rahlan drinking from me, and now I'm going to be thrown to a horde of ravenous vampires?

"She's already been drunk from today, so no more than two cups," Rahlan says.

The barman chuckles. "Blood is not worth silver. I'm offering thirteen pieces for alkema."

What?

The barman signals to someone behind us, and I whip around. A large bald vampire is heading right for me. I slide in front of Rahlan, using him as a shield. He grabs my arm and pushes me aside, not letting go this time.

To my relief, the bald vampire turns and heads down a corridor. The wrinkles on his face put him in his fifties, but his large body lacks the frailty that usually accompanies such an age.

I jump when the barman grabs my other arm. What the hell? Rahlan lets go, and I struggle against the barman's grip.

"Lord Rahlan?" I look up at him, but he ignores me. I'm his prisoner, right? Shouldn't I be in his custody?

Rahlan removes the bag from my back and frees me from the rope. Usually that would make me feel better, not worse. Why did he take it off?

He steps away from the bar, and the barman drags me off to the side.

"Lord Rahlan? What's happening?"

He finally makes eye contact but remains silent. I slam my fist against the barman's hand, but his grip doesn't falter. He forces me down the corridor, and soon a wall blocks my view of Rahlan and the other vampires.

"Rahlan!? Don't stand there! What's alkema!?" I shout.

The barman shoves me into a room. I hit the wooden floor hard, and the door slams shut behind me.

Chapter 7: Sold

I scramble to my feet and pull on the door handle. It won't budge. My arms ache from breaking my fall, but I push through the discomfort and bang on the door. "Let me out! I know you're-"

"Slave," a voice calls from behind.

My heart falls into my stomach. My body tenses, and I slowly turn around. The bald vampire is sitting on an old grey bed on the other side of the room. I'm trapped in here with him.

My senses are overwhelmed by the bedrooms putrid smell. Sunlight peeks through the cracks in the boarded-up window above the bed. His leather coat hangs over the lone chair in the corner.

I'm frozen.

"You appear confused," he says, feigning concern with a hint of malice hidden underneath. "'Tis cute."

He rises to his feet, and I step back. He approaches, and my back presses flat against the door. There's nowhere to go. He is huge – a head taller than me, with arms almost the size of my legs.

"You're flustered," he says. "Is it... desire?"

I jerk away as his grubby fingers reach for my hair.

His expression hardens. "Kneel, slave."

No. I shake my head, trembling.

His fist slams into my stomach, crushing my abdomen between his knuckles and the door. I fall to the ground and gasp for air. My arms snap to my middle as the pain radiates through my core. His blow reignites the bruises from Rahlan's assault.

"Your head says no," he begins, "but your breathing is more honest."

I push myself to sit up, keeping my balance with one arm and holding my burning stomach with the other. My neck cranes to meet his gaze.

"Lucky for you, disobedient human whores are my favorite."

No. Not this.

"Your kind needs to learn where they belong." He grabs my arms and throws me face first on the bed. The impact sends a new shock of pain through my stomach. I try curl up to protect myself, but he flips me on my back and wraps his fingers around my neck. I can barely get any air in. I pull against his grip, but it's fruitless.

He leans over me, and the bed sinks with his weight. "Don't worry," he says. His fingers curl under my pants' waistband. I hate the feeling of his rough skin against mine. "You'll enjoy this, whore."

No. I grip my pants with both hands.

He yanks hard, and my belt bites into my skin, making me groan. I try dislodging his fingers, but he grabs my wrist instead. My neck is released so he can catch my other wrist and force them together.

I try desperately to pull my hands apart. He wraps a finger around each wrist to hold them stationary with just one hand, trapping both my arms above my head.

He yanks at my pants again. I can't get my arms free. I squirm under his grip, jerking my whole body from side to side. Anything to keep his hands off me.

He yanks again, my belt snaps and my pants tear.

"No!"

He rips them further, tearing them completely off. Cold air rushes over my skin.

He straddles me, trapping my legs under his heavy body. I lift my head, and my breath catches in my throat. My shoes and underwear are the only clothing left below my waist.

His nails scrape against my skin as he grabs my shirt. One hard pull tears my shirt off my body, leaving just my bra behind.

"You are lucky that you were even allowed to live," he says. "Welcome to the rest of your pathetic miserable life."

He presses his legs between mine, forcing them apart. I turn my head and shut my eyes. I shut out the world around me. I don't want this. I don't want this. I'm not here. It's not real.

"Look at me."

I stay still.

"Look at me!" He yanks my hair, making my scalp sting.

My eyes open, focusing on the rotting wooden ceiling and letting his face remain a blur.

"Beg."

What?

"Beg to be defiled, whore!"

Tears well up in my eyes.

He pulls my hands back down to my stomach, and a hard slap hits my face.

"Beg me! Beg me to take you!" He slaps my stinging cheek again. I can't take this anymore. I can't. He ripped up my clothes. I'll be like the humans by that corner table. It's going to be like this forever. Tears roll down my cheeks, and I start to cry.

He pulls my hair to cause me further pain. I sob aloud, not caring who hears. I've got nothing left.

He slaps me again, and again, and again. I cry louder and louder, keeping my eyes closed.

He releases my wrists and jumps off the bed. I snap my legs together and curl up into a ball.

His arms wrap around my small form and lift me into the air, pressing me against his chest.

"You crook!" the man shouts. His voice isn't above me, it's below. I open my eyes. The bald man is on the floor, struggling to get up without tripping over himself.

Who's holding me? I don't need to look up. I recognize the leather coat. It's no knight in shining armor. It's no hero. It's Rahlan, the vampire who decided I was worth less than a horse.

I curl into myself and hide my eyes behind my arm. Maybe they're right. Maybe this is my place in this new vampire world. A new wave of tears washes over me, and I press my face into my arms.

Rahlan wraps his dark cape over me, shielding my body from the outside world. I bob up and down with his rhythmic steps. The tobacco smoke and incomprehensible murmuring returns as he steps into the bar section of this wretched place.

"Return the silver," the barman says.

Rahlan adjusts his posture to hold me with one arm. The coins jingle as he drops them on the bar counter.

Sunlight pierces through my cocoon's threading as he steps outside. The gravel crunches beneath his feet, and the smoky smell fades away.

What's next? Am I going to be fed to wild animals, or be used to test a sword's sharpness? I don't even want to know what awfulness awaits me.

He walks further before placing me on a log. The sharp bark irritates my backside. His cape is pulled away, exposing me to everyone. My eyes stay shut. I don't want to know how many vampires are watching me sob in my pathetic state. I can't stop whatever he wants to do to me, but at least I can spare myself the torture of watching it unfold.

The jeers don't come. It's almost silent other than chirping birds and the occasional gust of wind.

I peek my eyes open. The world is blurry, but the blotches of green leaves mean that we're far from the trade post. It's a forest, and it's just the two of us.

He steps back, and my gaze drifts to the dead leaves by my feet.

I hug my bare middle. Why couldn't Jacob be here instead of this vampire? There were many tearful nights when Mom passed on.

Jacob was always there for me, especially when times were tough. I need him now more than ever.

Rahlan holds out an apple for me to take, but my gaze lingers on the leaves below. The bald vampire's words play over and over again in my head – 'slave, pathetic, lucky to be alive'. I've never felt so low.

I watch the leaves dance in the wind. My sobbing dies down as time passes. The forest is peaceful, a beautiful place untouched by man or vampire.

"Do you have the strength to stand?" Rahlan asks.

I rise up on shaky legs. His hands snap to my side to help me up, and I cringe at the feeling of his cold fingers on my skin.

He quickly steps back, noticing my discomfort. He gestures for me to follow him.

The leaves crunch under our feet as we continue north through the forest. My stomach aches from the fresh assault, and we've adopted a slower pace to compensate. He took the bag instead of forcing me to carry it, and he left my arms free. Maybe he thought I'd lose it if he bound me now.

It plays over and over in my head. That man. That place. Rahlan.

"How could you do that?" I spit, "Was kidnapping me, beating me and leeching my blood not enough?"

His gait doesn't falter. He's not bothered.

"You're a monster," I mumble under my breath.

He grabs my arm, forcing me to my toes. "Grow up. You're a slave. I couldn't care less."

I return his glare. His eyes run up and down my body, before letting me back on the ground.

* * * * * * * *

The forest opens up to badlands with rolling rocky hills. Night falls, and we stop at a small cave. I take the nearest rock as my seat, not wanting to spend another minute standing. We've been walking over sharp rocky hills for hours, and my feet are killing me.

He unrolls his sleeping pouch but makes no effort to start a fire. I begin collecting kindling off the ground, figuring I'll need it more than him. Sticks and dry leaves are few and far between in this desolate place.

"There'll be no fire tonight," he says.

"I'll build it myself," I say without pausing my search.

He grabs my arm, making the kindling fall to the ground. "No fire."

"Why?"

He clenches his jaw, annoyed that I question him. "It draws attention."

Just like the candle's flame drew him to me. I rip my arm away from him and find a nook in the cave wall.

The temperature is rapidly dropping due to the absent sun, and the cold air nips at my exposed skin. I lean against the rock and hug my abdomen to try retain some heat. I'm in nothing but a bra, shoes and underwear. My knees curl up close, and I rub my sides up and down.

"Why do you do that?" Rahlan asks from his fluffy sleeping pouch.

"To warm myself up."

"Is it working?"

I ignore his taunt and nudge further into the rock.

"Come here," he says, sitting up right.

I approach with one arm holding the other. Am I in trouble?

"Get in."

What?

He pulls up the edge of the sleeping pouch, making room for me beside him.

I hesitate. His hand holding it open reveals its white fluffy wool. It looks warm, soft and cozy. I bite my lip and eventually convince myself to crawl inside.

I've never felt bedding like this, soft as a kitten's fur. It must've cost a fortune.

There's barely enough room for the both of us, and he takes up the large majority. His leather coat is pressed up against the length of my body. I'm a little squashed, but it's incredibly warm in here. I snuggle deeper into the pouch, bringing the rim up to my nose. This is nice.

It begins to dawn on me that I'm snuggling up against my captor. The thought would've petrified me a few days ago. Though he's not reluctant to beat me, he has never attacked me in my sleep. I suppose I trust him a little.

He said he doesn't care about me, but he's sharing his pouch, and he changed his mind about selling me. It's been on my mind for hours.

"I was just wondering... why did you come back?" I ask.

The night is silent, no insects chirp in this rocky place.

"I heard you," he finally says.

That wasn't what I meant, but his reluctance to answer makes me refrain from prodding further.

Chapter 8: Murder

I'm awoken by a shuffling behind me.

"What's going on?" I try sit up in the sleeping pouch, but he rests his hand on my head.

"Shh," he says. I lay back down, and he keeps his hand on me as he climbs out the pouch.

I pull it tight around my frame before the cold air rushes in. It's late in the night, almost dawn, and my eyelids feel like they're glued together.

He fishes out a brass contraption from the bag and takes a seat on a nearby rock. Bringing the crescent-shaped device to his eye level, he peers through its sights. His finger clamps the small string hanging off the side, and he marks a reading on the rock.

Unable to contain my curiosity, I crawl out the pouch and stumble towards him in my tired state. The chilly air makes my skin feel like I've just dived into a lake. I take a seat next to him and curl into a tight ball to retain some warmth.

"What are you doing?" I ask with a yawn.

"Plotting our course."

"With that thing?"

"It is a sextant," he says, "It measures the positions of celestial bodies."

"The stars?"

He peers through its sights again and marks another reading on the rock.

"But how can the stars..." I trail off.

"Here," he closes my hands around it and lifts it to eye level. "Don't drop it."

I nod.

"Close one eye and line up both sights with Iotl High."

"Itol High?"

"Did your father not teach you basic navigation?"

"I didn't know him." He died before I was old enough to remember.

Rahlan leans in close and wraps his arm around my shoulder. "See those two star clusters?" He points at the sky. "There are two twinkling stars between them, all on their own, Iotl High and Iotl Low."

"Two stars with the same name?"

"The story goes that they were once one, Iotl, but she split in two from sorrow."

"Sorrow?"

"They say Iotl was once with the west cluster, but she fell in love with Nidon, a star from the east. They were to unite half way between them, but on the way there, Nidon died from the cold, and Iotl found herself alone in the middle."

That's tragic. The frigid morning air makes me shiver. My breath blooms in front of me, fogging up the sextant's sights.

A heavy weight lands on my shoulders. It's his leather coat. I thread my arms through the sleeves and button up the front. It's so big that my fingers barely poke out the ends.

I look up at him. His black buttoned shirt is much more prominent.

"That should help you hold the sextant steady," he says.

I nod with a small smile. On him the coat only went to his thighs, but on me it reaches down to my shins. It's lined with a soft wool-like material on the inside. The chest area is almost large enough to fit two of me. He must've had it tailored to him, and it must've cost a fortune.

I press my arms against my midriff, pushing the cold air out and allowing the fabric to make better contact with my skin. It's not as warm and fluffy as the sleeping pouch, but it's a hundred times better than being in just a bra and underwear.

Another star catches my eye, "What about that bright one in the east cluster?"

"That's Icar, the warrior." He shows me how to calculate our location with the stars, and he shares their stories until they're hidden by the blue morning sky. I didn't think that vampires would concern themselves with such things.

* * * * * * *

After a few hours of traveling, we encounter a river. The Gaultane is still at least a day's journey away, and this one is far too thin to hold the Gaultane's reputation. The raging waters have worn away the rocks, leaving huge boulders sprinkled around its banks.

The rope is tied around my waist once again, but he left my hands free. I know better than to try take it off. He left his coat on me to protect me from the elements, and it provides padding which makes carrying the backpack far more comfortable. His coat is threaded with an intricate pattern of interlocking circles. I've made clothes before, but this work is well beyond my ability. It's not something a commoner could afford.

"If you're a lord, why do you travel alone? Where are your soldiers?" I ask.

"I don't have any," he says.

A lord without men? "But how do you protect your land?"

"I'd imagine my lands are now occupied by others."

"Wait... how can you be a lord without any land?"

"I campaigned for land and power, but one day something changed, and it all seemed so... frivolous." He glances down at me. "The world is cruel. You should come to terms with that. It'll save you needless suffering."

"What changed?"

"I suppose my title is no longer fitting. Old habits," he says, ignoring my question.

I don't pry further, sensing he doesn't want to share more.

We step through a clump of dense vegetation. Our waterskin is empty, and the sloshing river is calling me. Having my blood siphoned this morning has aggravated my thirst. "Can we take a brea-"

His hand clamps over my mouth, cutting me off and pulling me back into him. My eyes widen to the size of saucers. He's focused on something in the distance. I follow his gaze across the horizon. There's a pair of men, human men.

My heart drops into the pit of my stomach. I need to warn them before they share Neil's fate.

He presses my body against his, keeping my mouth shut with no room to move back. My hands snap to his, and I dig at his fingers. The old gag appears in the corner of my vision. Crud.

I bite down, and he rips his hand away with a grunt. Taking a huge breath, I scream at the top of my lungs, "Vampire! Run!"

Both men look directly at us. They bolt. Rahlan pushes me aside and takes off after them. I land painfully on all fours, almost falling flat on my face.

The men run in opposite directions, and Rahlan chases the one heading to the river. I drop the backpack and run after him.

Rahlan's much faster than the man, like a lion chasing down his prey. I'm left in the dust. I won't reach them in time. My shoes scrape over the dirt as I make a sharp turn, narrowly avoiding a pit. They're shouting. I run as fast as my feet can carry me.

The man falls to the ground by the riverbank, and Rahlan stands over him with his sword drawn. "Where is he!?" Rahlan shouts, "Where's Ivan the Huntsman!?"

"Please, I don't know what you're talking about," the man begs.

My legs burn as they push for the final stretch. I'm out of time. I charge into Rahlan's back, knocking him off balance. He hits the ground, and my body lands on top of his.

The man scurries to his feet, and Rahlan shoves me off, sending me rolling over the dirt. I let out a groan from my aching everything. The man dives into the raging river, and Rahlan comes to a screeching halt at the riverbank.

"Mark my words, monster!" the man shouts as the torrent of water pulls him away, "We will drive you out this land! Glory to the Huntsmen! And long live Ivan!"

Uncle Ivan?

Soon he's out of sight, but his voice continues to taunt Rahlan. "I hope we meet again, monster! Thank your lady friend..." his shouts fade behind the noise of the current.

Before I can fully process what's happened, Rahlan has his hand on my chest, lifting me up by the coat with my feet dangling beneath me.

"You stupid girl."

His grip forces my head up towards the sky, compressing my airway. "He was a-a Huntsman," I choke out, unable to take a full breath, "a hero."

"A hero!? You think the Huntsmen are heroes!?" He drops me, and I land hard on my butt.

"They defend those who can't defend themselves, and Ivan's a good man," I snap back.

His full attention lands on me. Malevolence radiates off him. "What did you say?"

The blood drains from my face. "They defend those who can't defend themselves."

"No," he shakes his head in disbelief, "You said Ivan's a good man. You know him."

"No, I-I've just heard stories." I don't want to find out how much anger he'd take out on Ivan's niece.

"There are no stories."

"I-"

"How do you know him? Are you one of them?" He glances at the backpack I left behind. "No. You're far too useless to be a Huntsman. Simple navigation eludes you." He rests a hand on the hilt of his sword. "What is your connection to Ivan?"

He sees right through me. My tongue is stuck in my throat. Trying to defend myself while I'm flustered will just dig a deeper hole.

He grabs my arm and pulls me close. "I find that pain loosens a stiff lip."

My mouth makes a thin line. I will die by his sword before endangering the little family I have left.

His hand curls up into a fist. I shut my eyes and tuck my head into my shoulder. My body tenses, and I try shield my middle with my free arm. The bruises are nowhere near healed.

My torso curls away from him. I can't stop myself from trembling. My legs will buckle the moment he hits me. The best I can do is hold still and mentally prepare myself for the impending assault. I'll endure the burning pain in my middle a hundred times before helping a vampire hunt down family.

His grip remains tight, but the blow doesn't come. I slowly peek open my eyes and meet his gaze.

He pushes me back, and I hit the ground again.

"It matters not." He smirks. "I have plans for you, friend of Ivan."

I shudder. He grabs the waist rope, forcing me to jump to my feet and follow after him. We trace our steps back to where we first saw the men. Their things are scattered around the area that was once their campsite. I let out a breath of relief knowing that his attention has shifted off me. There's smoldering ash and a sweet aroma from a meal they just ate. I keep my eyes open for any leftover food.

He finds a satchel lying in the long grass. It has a bow insignia embossed on its leather cover. Jacob has an iron necklace with the same symbol. He said that Ivan gave it to him as a gift, but he didn't mention it was a Huntsmen's mark. He joined the Huntsmen without telling me?

Rahlan flips the bag upside down, depositing its contents on the dirt. There are clothes, some wrapped spices and cotton paper. He picks out the paper and unfolds it to reveal a letter. His eyes scan the page, and his lips curl up into a grin.

I lean forward to get a view, but a dark glance tells me to back off. He stares at it for a minute before folding it up and placing it in his pocket. I want to ask him what it says, but it's better that his attention stays far from me.

* * * * * * *

We cross the river at a narrow point, boulder hopping to avoid soaking our clothes. Night soon falls. We've been walking through fields of tall grass for hours. He's not slowing down, and I'm exhausted, but I keep it to myself, not wanting to remind him of my presence.

After another hour of trudging through the grass, my legs are aching, but his gait shows no sign of fatigue. I'm not built like him. I bet he'd have dived after the man in the river if he wasn't tethered to me. I will ask politely.

"Lord Rahlan, are we going to set up-"

"Shh," he interrupts me.

I'm not trying to cause trouble, but my body can't keep up at this pace. "Can we-"

"Shut up." His eyes convey that that was the final warning. He unsheathes his curved sword, and I stumble back. I thought we were past the threat of him chopping me up?

He yanks on my rope, making me yelp and fall by his feet.

"Show yourself!" he shouts, scanning the direction we came. We're not alone?

Chapter 9: Ravagers

Quiet as a mouse, I slowly rise to my feet. His hand is gripped tight around the rope, leaving less than a foot between us. Whatever's out there - it wants to pick me off.

I scan the long grass, but there's nothing. It's a dark moonless night, and I can only hear my breath.

A gust of wind hits, and the air over my ears is deafening. It could use the noise as cover to sneak up behind us. I whip around, but there's nothing.

A twig snaps, and I almost jump out of my skin. That wasn't us. Something's out there, and it's close. I never thought I'd be so thankful that Rahlan is standing beside me. He'll kill it.

I follow his gaze back to our trail. The wind blows again, making the long grass move in waves. It reveals a dark protuberance behind the stalks, and my heart stops. It slips out of view the second I spot it.

An eerily cackle breaks the silence, and a dark figure rises from the grass where I stood just moments ago. I step back beside Rahlan.

The figure has long uncut hair. It obscures his face, but I catch a glimpse of his eyes – red. He's a vampire, but his body is crooked, and his skin is dry and sunken into his skull, not allowing his lips to meet.

"All of you," Rahlan says.

The figure spits on the ground, making me flinch. Out of nowhere, another one rises. Dark hair and crooked figure, just like the first. They're joined by a third, and I gulp.

Rahlan points his sword in their direction.

"We don't want you," the figure hisses. His scratchy voice sounds like he's smoked tobacco for decades. "We're just here... for a snack," he clicks his tongue on the k and his gaze lands on me, sending a chill down my spine.

"Get lost," Rahlan spits.

The figure takes in a breath and draws his short sword. "Your choice."

Rahlan's hand lands on my shoulder, and the other two circle around us, positioning themselves on all three sides. Their gait is uneven and unnatural, like they don't have full control over their muscles.

Rahlan keeps two in his view, his gaze alternating between them. I stand with my back to his, watching the third. I fish the metal eyeball flask out the bag on my back. The thought of it disgusts me, but I couldn't care less at the moment. It's better than nothing.

The one facing me draws his sword and bares his jagged teeth. It wants to bite me. I shudder and tighten my grip on the flask.

One charges. Rahlan shoves me to the ground and lunges to the left. The figure runs between us, and Rahlan strikes his back. He shrieks and waves his sword, but Rahlan parries and kicks him back.

The man regains his balance and shoots forward. Their blades meet again. Rahlan weaves his curved blade around the man's sword and rips it out his hands.

Cold fingers wrap around my arm and yank me back. I scream and flail, losing my grip on the awkwardly shaped flask. Rahlan whips around and swings his sword just over my head, making the monster hiss and let go.

He drives it back, but the third is charging from his blind spot.

"Behind you!" I shout.

Rahlan jumps to his left, and the man strikes the place where he once stood, almost as if he didn't see the movement. Their eyes lock and their blades meet. Rahlan wraps his curved sword around the man's blade and disarms him too.

The figures back off and group together. One still has his short sword, but the other two have to resort to their daggers. One of them is holding his arm – an injury from Rahlan's blade.

"Why draw this out?" one says, "There are three of us. You will fall. Give us the girl, and we will be on our way."

"Perhaps you will be victorious," Rahlan says, "but I'll take at least one of you down, maybe two. 'Tis a high price for a human."

They mumble to each other. My gaze is locked on them, and my heart is banging against my chest.

The one chuckles, "These are our parts."

"We'll be gone soon."

The crooked vampires turn to each other, mumbling something too soft for me to hear. They give each other one last look, then with a menacing glare in our direction, they slip back into the long grass, disappearing just as fast as they appeared.

Rahlan waits, listening for some time. I stay dead still.

He sheaths his sword, retrieves the flask and grabs my rope. I can finally breathe freely. He must be sure that there's some distance between us and them. I stick to his side as we continue to weave our way through the field, looking back every few seconds out of paranoia.

"Do I get a thank you?" he says with a smirk.

"Thank you for keeping my blood to yourself," I say with a sarcastic tone. I'm glad that I'm his captive instead of theirs, but I'm not going to genuinely thank him for it.

"They do not desire your blood."

What?

"They're ravagers. They crave bone marrow."

A shiver crawls down my spine. They were going to kill me and crack open my bones? The thought that they wanted to take something so deep within me is extremely disconcerting. I lose blood every time I'm injured, so I know I'll be fine as long as Rahlan doesn't drink too much, but my body would be unrecognizable if they took my bones.

I raise my gaze to him. Does he want my bone marrow too? Is it some kind of delicacy to them?

"You don't..." I trail off, unsure of how to ask.

"Don't fret, I have no desire to end up exiled as a ravager. Human marrow addiction cripples us, deforming our bones and degrading our eyesight."

I let out a silent sigh in relief.

"Thank you," I whisper.

He puts his hand on my head, and I swat it away. "Not funny."

I glance behind us again. It's all clear, but the thought that they could be there, just waiting for the opportunity to snatch me away, has my senses on overdrive.

I grab a piece of his cape and stick to him like glue.

"Scared?" he chuckles.

He may be an ass, but he's the ass who will protect me from those things.

After an hour of trudging through the long grass, it opens up to plains of tiny shrubs and weeds. The air is chilly now that the sun's lingering warmth has begun to fade. I'd be freezing if I didn't have Rahlan's coat.

Usually we'd be asleep by now. We're out in the open, with nothing for those demons to hide behind. Granted it's hard to see anything in the pitch-black night, but even my human eyesight would be able to spot something so large.

"Can we camp here?" I ask. I'm exhausted and my feet are aching.

"No, and for good reason," he says.

"We can sleep in shifts. My feet are on fire."

"Not an option."

I grind my teeth and continue trudging through the weeds.

Another hour passes and my legs are killing me. The ground is covered in tiny mole hills too small to see but big enough to force my feet into awkward uneven steps. Rahlan looks unbothered. He could go on for days.

A sharp pain rips through my leg, and I hit the ground with a groan. Curling it up to my chest, I rub it up and down, trying to massage the pain away.

My body is hoisted up in the air and pressed against his chest. His huge arms are holding me bridal style.

"Lord Rahlan?"

"There's no time," he says.

"My leg just-"

"I know."

I take hold of his shirt as an extra precaution. My gaze follows the buttons up to his formal collar. The stubble on his chin has morphed into a short dark beard over the last few days.

Letting out a yawn, I rest my head against his chest. The coat's thick leather and soft inner lining wraps tightly around my frame, keeping me warm.

The pain in my leg dissolves into a dull ache, but any attempt to move makes it flare up again. It's just a sore muscle. We've been walking since dawn. I'm used to traveling long distances to fetch water, gather wood or guide livestock, but humans aren't built to walk for sixteen hours without breaks.

Rahlan hasn't slowed down with the addition of my weight. In contrast, he's sped up. My slow pace was holding him back. Vampires are stronger and tougher. That's why their armies crushed ours. One vampire soldier is worth three or four humans.

I watch the terrain pass by as I lay comfortably in his arms, my eyelids growing heavy. I feel conflicted and confused. How many humans has he killed? I'd bet it's more than I can count on my fingers, yet I'm nestled against him without fear.

With another yawn, I let my eyelids slip closed. For the moment, I'm secure, and it's easier not to think too much about it.

* * * * * * *

"'Tis morning," Rahlan's voice brings me back into reality. I look up at him and rub the sleep out of my eyes.

He lets me down in an open field, making sure I can support my own weight before letting go. A jolt of energy runs through me at the sight of the river. It's huge - the Gaultane. The border to the vampire's country must be close, and... I follow the river trail with my eyes. The castle! Lord Guerin's castle, a human castle, right on alongside the river! It's just like the map said. If I can make it there, I'm free.

Rahlan's heavy hands land on my shoulders, and a shiver runs down my spine.

"Take a seat, breakfast," he says with a smirk.

I resist the urge to snap at him for addressing me as breakfast. He sits and forces me down with him. His arms snake around my chest, not giving me the slightest bit of wiggle room.

I suck in my breath and clench my jaw. This is the last one. In just an hour I'll be free, and my body and its blood will be for no one but myself.

He peels the coat away from my neck and bites down, making me hiss.

The minutes pass, my heart speeds up and my breathing quickens. He's close enough to feel my body's adverse reactions, but he couldn't be bothered.

He finishes up, and I rise on wobbly legs.

We head towards the river. I grab an apple from the bag on my back and take a bite.

"I'm not your breakfast," I grumble.

"You are my property. Your purpose is as I say."

Not for long. Falling a few steps behind him, I get to work on the knot holding this wretched rope around my waist. As long as it's slack, he won't notice a change.

I pull it a little too tight on accident, compressing my bruised middle. The sharp pain makes me stumble, and I bite my tongue to hold in a groan. My gaze shoots back to him. He hasn't noticed.

I let out a breath and try tying the rope again. My midriff is still sensitive from the beating he delivered the last time I tried to escape. There's a chance that I'll fail again and will be forced to endure his wrath a second time, but I don't have a choice. The border is just passed the river. Once I'm in their country, my chance of escape dwindles to nothing, and with it, the chance of ever seeing Jacob again. No one will help me. They'll consider me a slave or breakfast. My country is in shambles, but I can hide among the chaos. I need to stay in the land I know with the people I understand. This is my last chance to reach Jacob, and I can't let it pass by out of fear of failing.

Soon I've added a quick release to the knot. He won't notice the change without a close inspection, but just a tug in the right place will make it unravel.

Chapter 10: Lord Guerin's Castle

The raging water grows louder as we approach the river. The Gaultane's size and ferocity have earned it a dangerous reputation.

Rahlan scans the bank, looking for the best place to cross. "We'll head upstream for closer rocks," he says.

That'll take much longer than crossing over the castle's bridges. His decision to go out of the way to avoid it suggests that it's still under human control.

"We're not going to the castle?" I ask. It'll be suspicious if I don't acknowledge its presence.

"Maybe another time," he remarks as if it's an insignificant choice. My question makes me appear clueless, as if I think it's one of theirs.

We step closer to the bank, making it easier to travel. My eyes follow the turbulent water. I toss in a leaf, and it's immediately swallowed up below the surface, making me gulp. I can swim – in the calm shallow stream a half a mile from my village. This water is violent, unforgiving and nothing like the stream I know. I'll be swallowed up like that leaf. The possibility of drowning didn't cross my mind until now.

I lean over the water. The bank drops off like a sheer cliff. I have to do it. I'll never be free if I don't gather my courage. This is the path to reunite with Jacob. He's the last real family I've got left, and I'm not going to let him slip through my fingers.

I swing the bag off my shoulders and yank the quick release. The rope binding my waist falls to the ground, and I dive.

The freezing water hits my skin like a thousand needles. I'm swallowed whole. I can't see. Which way is up? My body tumbles through the raging current and slams against a hard rock, making me scream and lose my air. I paddle and kick and fight against the river with burning lungs.

I shoot out the surface and gasp for breath. Forcing my stinging eyes open reveals a huge wave about to hit.

I'm sucked back under and sent tumbling through the water. My arms and legs flail before I break to the surface again. Craning my neck to face up allows me to breathe. The waves obscure my vision and drown out all sound. My senses are overwhelmed.

The water dunks me under before letting me up again. Where's the castle? Is Rahlan waiting by the river's edge? I don't even know what direction I'm facing. The wild current drags me with no regard for my frantic movements, my arms unable to gain traction in its turbulent flow.

I slam into something solid. The jolt of pain makes me scream. My arms clutch at the hard surface, desperate to find a grip before the torrent washes me away. I wrap my fingers around a piece of vegetation and haul myself up.

Half my body is still submerged, but blinking my eyes allows me to see. I'm holding onto a root against a large boulder, right in the middle of the river. The combination of freezing water on my skin and adrenaline in my veins has me shaking.

I spot Rahlan sprinting alongside the riverbank, ending my short break before my muscles had a chance to recover. The boulder splits the river in two. One route carries the full force of the water, the other splits off into a calmer stream – the moat! It's the castle's moat!

I dig my fingers into the grimy stone and pull myself across to the stream. It's like the weight of the entire Gaultane is trying to squash me against this rock. With a groan and one final push, I'm flung back into the current. It carries me to the castle's side and the banks widen, spreading out its power so I can float without a fight.

The stone castle towers over me, engulfing me in its shadow. It didn't look so large from a distance. The walls are built from large yellow stones cut to fit perfectly with one another. The labor needed to construct such a structure is a testament to Lord Guerin's wealth.

"Oi! Look here fellas!" a man shouts from the castle wall. A wave of relief washes over me when I see he is indeed human. "We've been gifted a beautiful lass."

Gifted?

"Julia!" an angry shout follows from behind.

An arrow whizzes through the air, landing by Rahlan's feet. "Yield, vampire!" a man shouts from the castle gate. Two archers are stationed on the wall with bows drawn. Rahlan stops, resting one hand on his sword.

The gates fly open, and three men armored with wooly hide storm out with swords drawn. They stop at the moats edge, opposite Rahlan. I'm floating halfway between them.

"Julia," Rahlan growls, "Get back-"

"Is Lord Guerin here?" I ask the men, ignoring the vampire.

Two men chuckle, and the third pushes back his dirty brown hair. "Yep, ya' talking to him."

He's rough, unshaven, and has long hair - not what I expected for a lord of this land.

"You don't bear the same coat of arms?" I ask, glancing at the men's mismatching shields. If he's a lord, why don't his men wear his symbol?

"No time for chit-chat. Come here lass." He smiles, showing off his yellow teeth.

"Julia," Rahlan growls again.

Their uniforms don't match. Where's the chainmail that I've seen other lords wear? They don't bear the coat of arms painted onto the very castle they defend, and what did they mean by 'gift'?

This isn't Lord Guerin. These are bandits.

My stomach roils. They'll kill me.

I lunge for Rahlan. Both him and the men charge into the river from opposite sides. My arms slash through the water, propelling my body forward with uneven strokes.

A high-pitched whistle rushes over my ear and splashes just an inch from my face. They're shooting arrows at me! They'd rather I die than escape their grasp.

The men's splashes are gaining on me. I stretch my hand to Rahlan's. He's just out of reach. A hand lands on my shoulder and forces me under.

The weight keeps me down, and the water turns red. Is it me? The aching from the river's assault would hide any new injuries to my body.

The weight disappears, and I shoot to the surface and gasp for air.

The retreating men leave a red trail in their wake. Rahlan has one hand clasped around my arm and the other around his sword. An arrow grazes my coat, narrowly missing my skin. Another lands just inches from my face, floating back to the surface after the river absorbed its power.

Rahlan yanks me to his chest, using his body to shield me. His arms move in huge strokes, propelling us through the water to the moat's outer edge.

More arrows whizz past, splashing all around us. Rahlan grunts and pushes me up the bank before climbing up himself.

We run. He keeps my hand locked in his, pulling me forward so fast that I almost trip.

Soon we're out of the archers' range, but we don't stop until we're through the tree line and out of their sight. We weave our way deep through the forest, making it impossible for them to pursue us with any reasonably sized force. Rahlan keeps his grip on me, as if I'd have second thoughts about choosing him over them.

Satisfied that we're hidden, we slow to a stop, and he releases my hand. I double over to catch my breath.

The sight ahead makes me gasp. "There's an arrow in your shoulder."

Chapter 11: Injured

His gaze lands on me, and he straightens his spine. He pinches the arrow by the stem and slowly pulls it out with a circular motion. I wince just watching the painful-looking movement, but he doesn't flinch, and his expression shows no hint of discomfort.

The arrowhead is coated in blood, but it's intact. He rolls his shoulders like he's exercising a stiff muscle.

"Are you okay?" I ask.

He snaps the arrow, and the pieces fall out his hand. "Are you going to claim you slipped?"

I avert my eyes. He was hurt because of my actions. I didn't mean for harm to come to him. I was supposed to find sanctuary with Lord Guerin, and that would deter Rahlan from trying to recapture me.

A skirmish wasn't part of the plan, and neither was me fighting to reunite with him.

"We are not so fragile, like you humans." He unfastens his soaking cape and twists it in his hands. "You will be punished for that little escape attempt."

My stomach flips. I knew that this was the consequence of choosing him over the bandits, but the weight of my decision is only now starting to register. I'm reminded of his boot slamming into my middle, waves of pain following each blow. A feeling so intense that I'll writhe and crawl and beg and scream to get away.

What if it's worse this time? What if he breaks my fingers, like he came so close to doing before? My legs feel like they're about to fall out from under me. Without my fingers, I'll be helpless for months, maybe years. Just eating an apple on my own will be impossible. I'll be reduced to nothing but a blood bag. I can't take that. I can't.

My arms retreat back through the coat's huge sleeves, leaving them empty. I clamp my fingers under my arms for protection. I know that he has to punish me for what I did, but breaking my fingers is unnecessarily cruel.

He steps forward and lifts my empty sleeve. "What are you doing?"

I shut my eyes and squeeze my arms tight under my coat. Revealing my fear may encourage him to enact it. He wants to punish me. He wants to create a deterrent.

"You continue to test my patience. I'm sick of your schemes." He yanks me forward by the sleeve, almost causing me to lose my footing. His fingers move to unthread the coat's buttons.

"No." My legs collapse, and I fall to the ground. My body compresses into a tight ball, with my fingers hidden in the middle. His heavy leather boots are well within range of my head. "Just kick me now and get it over with."

He stands frozen, analyzing me. I don't dare look up. He can't be reminded of my fingers. If I stay by his feet, far away from his precise hands, his assault may not progress past blunt force. It'll still be hell, but it's better than the alternative.

"What are you hiding?" he spits, becoming more and more irritated by the second.

There's no reasonable explanation. Hiding my hands was a mistake. I should have just stood frozen and prayed that his assault wouldn't progress that far.

He shoves me over. I try sit up, but his hand grips my collar and pushes me back down, forcing my back flat against the dry leaves and causing my hair to fan out in the dirt.

He undoes the buttons and pulls the coat open. I clamp my arms down tighter, hiding my delicate fingers underneath. It's a superficial protection. He could so easily yank my arms up with his immense strength. My eyes mist over, and the trees overhead begin to blur with the sunlight.

His brows relax back to normal. My whole body is trembling, and my breathing is erratic. His eyes run up and down my body, pausing at the bruising on my abdomen from his last punishment.

"Julia," he sighs, "you need not hide your hands. I will not injure you."

If that's true, then it shouldn't matter if I keep my arms folded.

He buttons up my coat again, allowing my muscles to relax a little. My fingers aren't in immediate danger.

His hands wrap around my arms through the coat's leather fabric, and I'm lifted to my feet again. He wouldn't help me stand just to send me back down with a punch. I'm safe for the moment.

"Your escape attempt is not pardoned," he says, reading my expression. "There will be consequences, though there are more pressing matters than your discipline at this moment."

I stay still and silent, keeping my gaze down and my fingers protected under my arms.

He points east. "Walk."

The arrow penetrated his shoulder, but his arm moves like nothing even happened. Is he bleeding down his back? I peer around him to try get a view.

"Now," he growls, making me flinch.

I spin around and start walking.

My worn shoes trudge through the brown leaves, avoiding the shrubs and thorny bushes. My coat is still dripping. Its waterlogged inner lining prevents my legs from drying. I pick the damp leaves and dirt out of my hair as we walk, but my wet legs seem to pick up more than I can pull off.

We clear the tree line, revealing the backpack which I abandoned. Its contents are spewed across the riverbank where I made my leap.

We stop upon reaching the items. The sextant sits among the glass vials, and the eyeball flask lays by my feet. The thought of its contents makes me want to gag.

"Give me your hands," he says.

I avert my eyes, keeping my fingers hidden under my coat.

His face forms a scowl. "Julia, I have not much more patience to spare."

"I-" I try speaking, but I choke. I don't want to anger him, but I can't give him my hands. With eyes downcast, I hug myself tighter. It's as far from a combat stance as it could be. I'm not challenging him. My hands stay under my arms not out of disobedience, but out of fear of losing them.

He lets out a breath, whether it's from anger or disappointment, I don't know.

He unbuttons my coat once again, and my body tenses. I keep my hands under my arms, and the cold air makes me shiver.

He tugs on my wrist, and I jerk away from him.

"We've done this a thousand times," he says, "You will not be harmed."

The rope is in his hand. He's just going to tie me up, that's all. I cling to his words from earlier. If he was going to hurt me now, he wouldn't be asking me to comply.

After a moment of hesitation, I untuck my hand from its protective cocoon. He threads my arms back through the sleeves and behind my back. I suck in a breath. He won't harm me, I repeat in my head. The rope binds each of my wrists to the opposite elbow, rendering my arms useless like before.

Balancing is now front and center in my mind. If I fall over, it'll hurt, and I won't be able to get up without his assistance.

He collects his various traveling possessions off the bank and packs them in the bag. It gives me a much-needed break from his attention, and I'm feeling much more secure now, which is somewhat ironic considering that I'm bound.

Once done, he hangs the bag on my back and buttons up my coat.

He loops the rope around my neck.

"What are you doing?" I blurt out, suddenly much more aware of my own mortality, "That's supposed to go around my waist."

"You've lost that privilege." He loops it around a second time and secures it with a knot under my chin. "Besides, I think this arrangement is much more suiting for someone of your status."

Privilege? I scrunch up my brow. "But what if I trip and you don't notice? I'll be strangled"

"Good point." He leans in. "Don't trip."

With that, he starts walking, and I follow, not having a choice.

The ring around my neck is too close for me to see, but I'm well aware of its presence. It's as if someone's hands are wrapped around my throat, ready to press down and cut off my airway. I'm collared like livestock, and the leash leads to his hand. Is it just to humiliate me? Does he think treating me like a domesticated animal will keep me docile? If anything, it has the opposite effect.

We boulder hop over a narrow section of the river. It's not long before Lord Guerin's former castle has vanished from view. We should be crossing the border soon, into the vampire country. Maybe we already have, but a truly hope not, though it seems inevitable at this point.

We hike for an hour over lumpy terrain. My coat has dried, but my shoes are falling apart. They're little slippers I made from cowhide. Built for working in the fields, they're not meant to travel cross-country.

We crest another hill and my heart drops at the sight. A huge city stands just a mile ahead, with walls so tall that I wouldn't think possible. It's built from thousands of small black bricks, completely foreign compared to the human architecture of natural stones to which I'm accustomed. It engulfs the surrounding land in shadow – a visual display of its overbearing presence. It's a vampire city.

Chapter 12: Caged

He pauses our march to gaze upon the city. "Magnificent, is it not?"

"That isn't the word I'd use," I say. It's befitting that a man who drains blood would live in a black city that drains life from the field around it. In his eyes it's a home, with huge brick walls and sentries for protection, but in mine it's a nest of vicious vampires that wish to crush me beneath their feet.

Our journey is over, and I fear what that means for me. The city which brings him comfort brings me distress. There's no reason for me to follow him through its gate.

I take a deep breath and muster my confidence. "This is where we part," I announce.

"Oh, is it?" He raises an eyebrow, not taking me seriously.

"Yes," I square my shoulders, "You're home. You don't need my blood anymore. I can go free."

"That's cute," he chuckles.

I glare at him. "Cute?"

"Your misunderstanding of the situation. 'Tis cute, almost childlike. Did you think I was jesting when I said I had plans for you, friend of Ivan?"

I gulp. He may be my Uncle, but I barely ever saw him. It was Jacob who visited him, not me. "I told you, I don't know him."

"Is that so?" He's not buying my lie in the slightest. "Then I suppose you have no further use to me. Fortunately, young women like yourself are the most popular choice for those who like to keep fresh blood on hand. There's a market in the city center, and I know you'll make a fine pet."

I shoot him a dirty look, and he smirks.

We continue our path towards the city. The huge black walls loom over us. They cast a shadow that envelopes our tiny frames well before we reach the gate. The city is huge, with red tiled roofs extending as far as I can see. I'm in a state of disbelief that walls of such immense height could circle such a large place.

The walls are joined by tall towers with round roofs. A crisscrossed metal grid hangs above the gate, ready to slam shut at a moment's notice. I can't imagine why they need such a large entrance. Its height could accommodate an elephant riding another elephant.

Two towers loom over us from either side of the gate, with slits in their walls to allow soldiers to peer out. Every edge is carved to be round. It looks nothing like any structure I've laid eyes on, and its foreignness serves as a reminder of how far I've strayed from home.

It's built to be impossible to siege, but at the same time, impossible to escape. Though I don't want to admit it to myself, I know that after I cross the gate's threshold, I'll never be able to leave of my own volition.

Nine armored guards linger by the entrance. Their huge builds leave no doubt in my mind that they're vampires. A few glance in our direction as we enter, but they show little interest. I doubt they'd be so apathetic if I tried to leave unaccompanied.

The houses inside are just as strange – built with wood and red tiled roofs, at least two or three stories high. They're all connected to each other, attaching to the city's walls wherever possible. Every edge is rounded, and the upper floors overhang the muddy street.

A robed vampire exits as we enter, and his gaze lingers on me as he passes by. I avert my eyes as I'm reminded of the rope around my neck. They must consider me no different from a mule with this bag on my back. In this city, I have the status of an animal, if not less. To the guards, I'm not a citizen of an enemy nation, I'm Rahlan's property.

The thought makes my heart sink. I used to be able to shrug off Rahlan's claims of ownership over me, but now it feels so much closer to reality. Before there was a rope standing between me and freedom, but now there's a fifty-foot wall and hundreds of armed guards.

I quicken my pace to walk beside Rahlan, hoping I'll appear a little more equal.

"Looking forward to your punishment? I know I am," he says.

"You take pleasure at the thought of me suffering?" I have far more reason to hate him then he has for me, yet I don't wish him pain. I just wish him to be somewhere very far away from me.

"I take pleasure in the thought of the obedient and mild-mannered human I'm about to acquire."

He tucks my hair behind my ear. I jerk back and mentally scold myself for not pulling away sooner.

"There are ample punishments that will not cause you harm," he says.

I hate how giddy he is about this whole thing.

"Can't you forgive me?" I ask, "I didn't mean for you to get shot."

"That blame does not rest on your shoulders. You did not draw the bow." He pauses. "Know that if you do try to injure me, I will return the favor."

I would never try to injure someone, except maybe for my own self-defense. I've been on the receiving end enough times to know that I wouldn't want to dish out such a horrible feeling. But if he doesn't consider it my fault, then why is he so insistent about making me pay?

"If you don't blame-"

"Your punishment is for trying to flee, again. That habit is becoming rather bothersome."

Is it possible to change his mind, or is a human's word just not worth consideration?

A figure in a second story window catches my eye – a human girl around my age in a frilly white dress. I'd expect humans trapped in a vampire city to appear more distressed, yet she seems almost disconnected from the world around her. Is she one of the pets Rahlan spoke of?

Her eyes look down on me with pity. I wonder if other vampires lead their captives around on a leash, or if it is-

Something hits my face, and it takes me a second to realize that I bumped into someone. A hand grabs my coat, and I'm flung back with incredible force. My bound arms are useless to break my fall, and my body hits the ground and rolls across the dirt road.

After a brief moment of wiggling, I resign myself to lay on the ground. It's impossible to sit up on my own.

I shake my head and try blink the dust out of my eyes. It was Rahlan who threw me like a dangerous snake. What did I do?

He has his back to me, and his hand on his sheathed sword. All his attention is on a man in a hooded robe – the man I bumped into. The man's slightly shorter than Rahlan, with a much slimmer build. No – it's a woman. Though I can't see her eyes, her pale skin and confident posture confirm that she's a vampire. No human would be so secure in such an evil city. Her lips part with a smile, baring her elongated canines, almost as if she's showing them off.

If she's trying to intimidate me, mission accomplished. I'm glad Rahlan is standing between us, especially since I can't even sit up.

The guards' pay close attention, ready to intervene if a fight breaks out. Rahlan's gaze is locked with the woman's, both of them waiting for the other to make a move.

A guard steps forward, and the woman breaks her death stare. She turns away and continues out the gate.

Rahlan pulls me to my feet. "Eyes forward when walking," he growls.

Who was she? He seemed more concerned there than he did when facing the ravagers.

He pulls the neck rope taut, keeping me less than a foot from him. I wish my hands were free so I could get this damn thing off.

We turn off the main road and head down a dimly lit alley. I resist the urge to gawk at the tall houses on either side of us out of concern that I'll bump into another psychopath. The one dragging me through here is more than enough.

He knows exactly where he's going, and the surrounding buildings are becoming more rundown as we walk. The front of the city displayed wealthy homes, whereas these shoddy wooden structures are crowded on top of one another. Where is he taking me? The possibility that he could inflict my punishment at any moment is an ever-present source of anxiety.

His hand wraps around my arm, and he leads me down a set of stairs at the base of a building. He's brought me to a grimy stone basement.

He forces me forward into a poorly lit passage, and I grit my teeth when the bars come into view. It's a dungeon. The passage is lined with cells on either side. A thick smell of mold overwhelms my senses.

The cells are divided into two, an upper and lower level, neither tall enough to allow prisoners to stand. There's no doubt in my mind that this place is meant for humans.

We reach the decaying wall which marks the end of the passage. He kneels to inspect the bottom cell. It's not much more than a square hole in the wall, with darkness obscuring its far end.

He removes the bag off my back and works on the knot by my chin.

"You're punishing me with prison? As if I'm a criminal?"

He frees me from the rope. "No. I have more important tasks to attend to."

The cold wet air makes me shiver. He leans his weight on my shoulders, and I ignore his hint to kneel. He presses his knees against mine, forcing me down and shoving me in the cell.

"But worry not," he says, "You will atone for your disobedience soon enough. Until then, self-reflection would be a good use of your time." He slams the barred door closed and turns the key, and the lock engages with a clunk.

His footsteps fade away as he exits the passage, and an eerie silence creeps in to take its place. The cell's stone ceiling is too short to stand, and it's only just long enough to lie down. The air is stale, and the wet stone walls are covered in a disgusting black grime.

The sunlight doesn't touch my cell. It's illuminated by nothing more than a dim glow reflected down the passage. This place is bare other than a bucket in the corner, and there's a suffocating atmosphere of rot and decay, like a tomb.

I stretch out my hand and test the bars. The door doesn't budge, and the keyhole is shielded with an iron plate to keep it out of my reach. The bars are embedded in the stone floor and low ceiling. I try rattle and twist each one, but none of them have even the slightest give. There's no getting out of here.

My cell is perpendicular to the passage, blocking my view from everything other than the empty cell opposite me.

"Hello?" I call, hoping for a companion in this dire situation.

No one answers. I'm alone in this place.

I pull the coat tight around my small form. The pressure gives me a sense of security, even if it is superficial. I've never been locked in a dungeon before. I'm a law-abiding citizen, yet now I'm treated like a criminal - no worse, like an animal. Rahlan's going to subject me to something horrible, and I have no power to stop it. He calls it a punishment, saying I must atone, as if this is some twisted form of justice. What laws have I broken? He has killed men for sport, yet there's no one to hold him accountable. He lives under the law of his king, but I live under the law of Rahlan – a place where my freedom can be taken away just for who I am.

I'm upset. I shouldn't let it cloud my thinking, but I can't help feeling discouraged by the situation. I'm locked in a cell, in a well-guarded city, further from my brother than ever before. It's almost nonsensical that I traveled such a long journey only to be trapped in a place too small to stand. If I hadn't been captured, I'd be in Fekby right now. I'd be with Jacob.

He will have heard of the loss of our village by now. He must know that something went wrong on my journey to meet him. What if he believes me dead? If he leaves Fekby without me, how will I find him? He's the only real family I've got left, and probably my only friend too.

No, I shouldn't worry. He's clever. He'll leave a path for me to follow, a message of some kind. I just hope he doesn't grieve as if I was lost.

Hours pass. The silence is interrupted only by dripping water and the occasional rat squeak. I search my cell the first time I hear it out of paranoia. Why would such a creature be down here? There's no food to steal.

Food. My mind has been on food for a while now. I haven't eaten since this morning, and that was only an apple. He wouldn't leave me down here to starve, would he? He needs me alive for his plan, but if he figured out another way to find Ivan, then what would happen to me? Would he even come back? There'd be no accountability, no punishment for him, other than maybe a fine for creating a foul stench in the dungeon.

I curl up in a ball in the center of my cell, bringing the coat's collar up to my nose. It's big enough to cover me head to toe if I tuck in my knees, and its inner woolen layer retains heat much better than the old linen shirt I had before. The thing which gives me the most comfort in this miserable place belongs to Rahlan.

Chapter 13: An Ally

My eyes peek open, and I'm greeted by the dingy cell, dimly lit by a thin streak of morning light. It's disappointing. I was hoping that somehow, through some sort of miracle, that I'd wake up at home in my familiar bed.

I unfurl from my sleeping ball. The stone is less forgiving on my back than Rahlan's pouch, but at least the coat offers a little bit of padding.

With a small pebble as my brush, the layer of grime on the walls acts as my canvas. I've never been much of an artist, but maybe whoever else ends up stuck in here will enjoy my crude drawings mocking these hot-headed vampires.

The hours drag on. My cell was built with one hundred and sixteen bricks, at least from what I can see. I counted three times to be sure.

There's no jailer, but someone has to come soon, right? I'm parched. The last time I drank was during yesterday's river adventure.

Rahlan locked me up in here in hopes that I'd fret over the punishment, but I refuse to let it occupy my mind. It's not like it'll help my situation, and I don't want to let him win.

Leather shoes tap down the stone passage. Someone's here. I perk up in excitement but resist the urge to call out. Until I know who they are, it may be best if I don't drag their attention.

The footsteps are light, different from Rahlan's heavy soldier boots.

A slim figure appears in front of my cage, and I retreat back into the shadows. To my relief, her back is to me. She's dragging a limp body - a human.

The vampire shoves the human in the cell opposite mine. The barred door screams closed, and the loud bang makes me jump. The lock clanks shut, and the vampire leaves as quickly as she appeared.

The body is as still as a corpse, but I know the vampire wouldn't bother locking up a dead person.

I creep forward on my hands and knees, getting as close as my cell bars allow. It's a human woman, just a few years older than me. She's covered in a ragged grey dress, and her boney frame suggests that food is scarce. Her long black hair is tattered and splayed over her face, like she's just been in a tavern brawl. I probably look just as disheveled.

I pull my knees in and rest my head against the rusty bars. Her chest rises and falls in a slow rhythm. How will she react to waking up in this dingy place? What if she starts screaming, bringing angry vampires upon us? Yesterday, I was hoping for a companion to comfort me, but now it looks like I may be the one doing the comforting. How can I reassure her things will be okay if I can't even reassure myself?

An hour later, she begins to stir. I perk up but quickly scoot back in my cell, hiding myself in the shadows. She could be crazy for all I know. I doubt being a prisoner is good for her mental stability.

"Ah hell." She bangs her arm against the bars, sounding more annoyed than anything else. I'm not sure if that means she's levelheaded or completely off her rocker. I'd freak out if I woke up here.

She pushes herself up and rests her head in her hands. Maybe I should give her time to recover before making myself known.

She rubs her palms in circles over her eyes, and her gaze lands directly on me. "Jaclyn, you?" she asks, startling me in the process. The darkness didn't hide me as well as I had hoped.

"I-I," my voice hitches. I hadn't realized how dry my throat was. "I'm Julia."

She yawns and scratches her head. "What's the time?" I didn't think it was possible for a human to be so relaxed under the vampires. Her calm demeanor makes me wonder if she's already familiar with this awful place.

"Noon. You've been sleeping there for the last hour." I'm just guessing based on how the streak of sunlight has receded out of my cell.

She lets out a breath and smiles like I made a joke. How can she be content with all of this? Maybe she's experienced it enough to know what to expect. Though I'd never admit it to Rahlan, the fear of the unknown has me on edge.

"Do you know what they have in store for us?" I ask.

She stretches her neck, trying to get a view of the adjacent cells. "That's a nice coat," she says.

"The uh... It belongs to the vampire who captured me."

She straightens her legs and leans against the cell wall. "You mean your master?"

"He's not my master."

"Oh really? You here for the scenery?" She gestures to the bars and moldy stone walls.

I avert my eyes and curl my knees closer to my chest. I'm not owned. I'm not a piece of property. He's not my master.

"Hey, don't take it like that," she says. "I envy you. I wish I had a master instead of a mistress, and based on that coat, it looks like he takes good care of you."

"Takes good care of me?" I furrow my brow. "He tried to prostitute me."

"Tried?" Her mouth hangs open. She probably thinks I fought him off. If only I was that strong. She beams like a child waiting to hear a story from their grandmother, but it's not one I want to share.

"He changed his mind," I mumble.

Her excitement fades at the realization that I was simply spared. Much to my relief, she avoids prodding further.

She shouldn't confuse Rahlan for a good person. "He still locked me up in here though," I add.

She smirks. "What'd you do?"

"Nothing deserving of this."

"Ah-huh." She picks at her teeth.

"My freedom was stolen. I was trying to get it back."

Her eyes widen. "And you're still alive?"

Rahlan needs me for more than just blood, but I don't know if I can trust this woman with that information. The less people who know about my connection to Ivan, the better. For all I know, the vampires could have a price on his head.

"Why would you rather have a master?" I ask, hoping to change the topic.

"The women are venomous."

My back stiffens against the wall. "Venomous?"

She pulls down her collar, and I take in a sharp breath. Her shoulder is black, with inky streams traveling down her chest like tree roots. They reach all the way to her left hand, threading between her fingers.

"It's usually deadly. I was lucky. You don't want to piss them off," she says. "As for why I'm here, it was a snarky comment."

I frown. "How long has it been?"

"I've been in Gilsa for a week, but I was taken two months ago."

"They invaded two months ago?" How did I not hear about it sooner? We could have fled long before they arrived at our village.

"They snatched me up well before the invasion began. I was collecting medicinal herbs near the border." Her eyes fall to her lap. "I didn't realize they were desperate enough to take people in broad daylight."

"Desperate?" How could such powerful creatures be desperate?

"You haven't heard? We've neighbored their country for a century, yet they've only attacked now. Surely you didn't think it was down to chance?"

I only learned of the invasion when they were upon us, and Rahlan brushed off my questions with condescending remarks.

She takes my blank expression as an invitation to continue. "They're vampires. As we keep cattle, they keep us. Something happened to their human population, so they've taken us to replace them, and since our numbers are in great excess to meet their needs, our lives are worth little."

She leans back against the wall, staring at the ceiling. "Apparently some human militia killed one of their lords on his own land. It gave them the excuse they needed for war. Other countries-"

The basement door flies open, making a loud clank as the handle hits the wall. Heavy leather boots strut down the passage. I know those arrogant steps anywhere.

Rahlan appears in front of my barred cell. The short beard which he grew on our journey has been shaved clean. "Ready to begin?" he says.

"Do I have a choice?" I ask.

"No. It's just a formality." He unlocks the cell. "Get out."

My stomach twists. Just a moment ago, all I wanted was to be free from this cell, but if that means facing the punishment, I wouldn't mind spending more time in here.

He won't wait for long. If I don't move, he'll drag me out. I take in a breath and crawl out the cell with as much dignity as I can muster. I square my shoulders and straighten my spine, feigning confidence in the hopes of not giving him any satisfaction.

He tosses a grey garment to me. "Change," he commands.

I run the old material through my fingers. It's ragged, coarse, and full of holes. "I'm happy in this," I say with a hand on my coat's sleeve.

Jaclyn watches from her cell with wide eyes like she can't believe the words coming out of my mouth.

"I bet you are happy in a lord's jacket," he says. "If you don't like your new clothes, you're welcome to display yourself to the city." His hand lands on my shoulder and clamps to the leather.

"Okay, okay." I try shake him off, but his grip stays tight. He's not letting go. I step closer to him to at least be out of Jaclyn's view before sliding out of the coat, but it's still embarrassing that she knows I'm in my underwear in front of him.

He folds the coat in his arms, seeming rather pleased to have it back – the coat which is apparently too good for me. Whatever.

I gulp down a drink from the waterskin and slip on the garment. It's an old loosely fitting dress made from scratchy material that irritates my skin. It's fit for a slave. I suppose it was only a matter of time before he dressed me to match my role.

He grabs my arm and marches me out of the dungeon. I shield my eyes from the bright sunlight. He shoves me up the main road, almost causing me to lose my balance a few times.

"I can walk without your man handling. Let-" my breath gets stuck in my throat at the sight before me. A gathering of vampires surround a wooden platform in the town square. It's a stage... with a pillory.

Chapter 14: Punishment

"Move it." Rahlan shoves me forward, breaking my trance. I instinctively pull back, like a deer being forced into a hungry pack of wolves, but he overpowers me with little effort. My feet stumble as I try to regain my balance.

We step into the square. It's a large muddy quad surrounded by tall buildings and thin roads trailing out in each direction. The top floors are painted white, and the ground floors are colored brown with mud.

Over twenty vampires surround the stage. All these people are here to celebrate my misfortune.

Only a few notice us as we approach the group. Maybe we'll settle among them? Could Rahlan have brought me here just to witness someone else's punishment?

We reach the base of the stage stairs, and a pit forms in my stomach. He forces me up ahead of him. The entire crowd's attention immediately lands on us, and my hope that this was just a threat evaporates.

Humans cower among the vampires – slaves brought to witness a demonstration of what would happen if they were as foolish as me.

A raised wooden board with three holes is mounted at the front of the stage. One large hole for my neck, and two smaller ones on either side for my wrists. A bulky vampire dressed in black armor stands beside the wooden pillory. He looks like an executioner who torments humans as a hobby.

Rahlan forces me forward. My nerves make me trip over my own feet, but his iron grip on my arm keeps me upright. All eyes are on me. I wish I could just evaporate into thin air.

The guard takes me from Rahlan, and it feels like the whole situation collides in on me at once. I'm in the hands of a malicious man in front of a heartless crowd.

He grabs my free arm and holds me in front of him, presenting me to the crowd. They cheer, like the guard is showing off his hunting prize.

The stage is only half a man's height, making my legs well within grabbing distance. More vampires watch from the top story windows, enjoying my conundrum from the comfort of their homes.

My heart pounds in my chest. It's like I'm a calf about to be sacrificed. A shiver crawls down my spine. I'll be completely helpless in that thing, at the mercy of this evil man. I twist my neck around and call for the one vampire I know – the one who can put a stop to this, "Rahlan! Lord-"

"Silence!" The guard shakes me back and forth, and the motion makes my brain bounce around my skull. Where is Rahlan? I can't see him. Did he just abandon me here to suffer at this man's hand?

"As you have witnessed," the guard announces, "this poorly mannered human knows not when to keep its mouth shut!"

Its?

"Today it will face retribution for failing to hold its tongue in the presence of its master!"

The vampires laugh and cheer, but the humans stay silent. The guard opens the wretched device with one hand while keeping me immobile in the other.

An enormous weight forces my head down, resting my neck in the largest of the three holes. More hands lock around my wrists and force them into notches on either side of my head. It's like he has a million arms to hold me down.

The top piece of wood slams closed, and the sudden pressure around my wrists and neck makes me panic.

"No!" I wail. My back is arched. I can't stand straight. I pull back against the holes on instinct, but my head is flush against the board. I can't see through my hair. Where's the guard? Rahlan can stop this. Where's he? "Rah-"

A handful of mud is squashed against my face. The irony dirt forces its way into my mouth and up my nostrils. I gasp for breath as soon as the guard removes his filthy fingers. The crowd laughs.

"Cud eater!" someone shouts. A ball of mushy liquid goo smashes into my ear. I shut my eyes and try wrench my hands back out of the wooden restraints. I twist and pull and twist, but nothing works.

Another ball of slime hits my head, sliding over my ear and down my chin.

Rotten fruit splats behind me, and the pips freckle my skin. I breathe from my nose, and the putrid smell hits me all at once. I gag, and someone takes the opportunity to land a balled mixture of dirt, rotten fruit and dung in my mouth.

The crowd cheers. I start to dry heave, but my empty stomach produces nothing. My teeth grit together in an attempt to keep anything else out.

A hand full of gunk lands on my nose and covers my eyes. It's the guard. He's the only one close enough to touch me. He runs his filthy hand up over my forehead and threads his fingers through my hair, soiling it down to the roots.

He takes another handful of gunk and presses it against my ear, running his fingers up through my hair. He's covering every inch of my head with the foul stuff.

His hands finally let go of my hair, no doubt changed from blonde to brown at this point. A ball of gunk hits a bruise on my stomach, making me wince. I'm pelted again and again.

"Disgusting!" someone shouts, and more gunk follows. I keep my eyes shut tight and try turn my head, but the board gives me no slack.

I breathe through my teeth, leaving just a narrow slit between my lips to allow air in. The smell is horrendous. Using my nose will make me sick.

"Spineless human!" More gunk hits my legs, and something gooey is smeared over my face.

"Not hungry, human?" The guard taunts. He pushes a handful of the gooey rotten food against my nose and between my lips.

I hold my breath. He eventually gives up trying to get it in my mouth, but my relief is short lived. He pulls back my collar and dumps it on the back of my neck.

The cold sticky liquid oozes down my back and around my torso, dripping down the inside of my dress. The crowd doesn't cheer with the same enthusiasm as before. Another clump of gunk hits my head, but all I hear is a low murmuring. At this point there's so much mud on me that I doubt they can see the difference.

The pelting becomes less and less frequent, and after an hour, it seems to be over with. The mud and dirt and dung and oil has caked over my face, sealing my eyelids shut. I can't hear the guard or the crowd anymore. I guess everyone left after growing bored of my humiliation.

My spine is arched at an awkward angle, and it's really starting to take its toll. Adjusting my feet provides no sense of relief. It's like this thing was designed to make its victim as uncomfortable as possible.

Hours pass, but the pillory doesn't allow my mind to wander. Standing hunched over provides enough discomfort to keep me grounded in reality.

Though my eyes are closed, I know the sun is setting if not already set. The previous warmth on my skin is now absent. It stayed long enough just to dry this crud on me.

A heavy footstep from behind makes me flinch. I've been alone on this stage for hours, but now someone's standing over me. Has the guard returned with a new appetite? My body tenses. How can this not be enough? Do I really have to endure everything again?

There's a loud click to my right. It's unlocked.

The top board is lifted away, and I'm finally released. I take a step back, but my legs give out, and I hit the wooden floor.

On instinct, I raise my hands to clean the hardened mud from my eyes, but I'm stopped by a heavy stick.

"Wait," a voice says. Rahlan.

I sit still, relieved that I'm in Rahlan's presence instead of the guard's.

A torrent of freezing water washes over me, and the cold shock makes me squeal. An empty bucket clunks as it hits the ground.

My eyes open to a blurry world. It's dark, early evening. A tall figure, Rahlan, stands over me.

"Up," he commands.

My legs are aching, and my mouth hangs open. I give him a blank look, too exhausted to form words.

"Up!"

To avoid a tiring argument, I follow his command and rise on wobbly legs. My vision comes into focus, and I stammer backwards at the sight that greets me. He's pointing his sword at my chest!

"Relax." He pokes me with the sword, but there's no pain. It's sheathed.

He presses it against my back and guides me towards the stage stairs. He's using it like a stick to avoid touching me. Ass.

I take the steps one at a time, being extra careful not to fall with my fatigued legs.

He uses the sword to guide me down a dimly lit road. The cold air has crept in. I hug my sleeveless arms to try retain some heat. The houses project candlelight on the street through doors and windows. They look warm and cozy, a sharp contrast to how I'm feeling.

While this experience was anything but pleasant, I'd endure it ten times over if it meant avoiding being beaten. I'm still bruised from his retaliation from the first time I tried to escape. At least this punishment didn't hurt.

A hazy mist emanates from a building ahead. We step inside. The walls, floors and low ceiling are all made of smooth beige stone, and the whole place is filled with steam.

Rahlan nudges me through a series of passages, finally stopping inside a small room lit by a single candle. It's a bath. The floor has a small ledge before dropping off into a pool of water – steaming water.

Rahlan removes his cape, wraps it around his sword and steps out of his huge boots. He unthreads the buttons on his shirt, revealing his muscular chest. No wonder he can overpower me so easily. He's stronger, faster and more resilient. It hardly seems fair. He has every possible advantage over me.

He unclips his belt, and I turn away.

There's a splash in the bath, but I keep my eyes down.

"You can look," he says, "'Tis safe."

I slowly lift my gaze to him. He's neck-deep, and the murky water hides everything below his shoulders – his huge shoulders.

"What's keeping you?" he asks.

Chapter 15: Bath

The steaming pool is built to fit ten people, but it's just the two of us. I gulp. It's not right for an unmarried man and woman to bathe together. But In his mind, he owns me. He could do whatever he wants without repercussions.

I kneel by the corner of the pool and splash some water over my arms and face.

"If you don't bathe properly, you'll spend another night in jail," he says, "I can't sleep near such a smell."

I rise to my feet and turn to the doorway. "I think I'll find another bath. This one's full of crap."

A hand on my dress pulls me off balance, and I go tumbling backwards with a scream. The water engulfs me whole, soaking through my soiled clothes in an instant.

I shoot to the surface and wipe my eyes clear. Rahlan is back in his corner.

"You're an asshole," I grumble.

"You behave like a child," he says.

"I do not!"

The corner of his lips curl up into a smirk. I fold my arms. Whatever.

"Disrobe," he orders.

"Get lost," I spit.

"Stop being difficult."

"Sorry, you're right," I say with a sarcastic tone, "I'm just being difficult not wanting to be nude in a bath with a man who would happily have me prostituted."

His mouth opens, but no words come out. He knows what he did was wrong. Even with his twisted form of justice, where kicking me while I'm down and locking me in a pillory is a fitting response for trying to get away, I'd done nothing to provoke him to sell me to a brothel. I followed his every command that day, and he threw me to the wolves.

"I made a mistake," he says, "You need not fear such a thing happening again."

I turn to face the wall. Venting my anger is the only easy way to talk about it.

His words do make me feel a little more secure. I pull the soaking dress over my head and place it on the ledge.

My hands rest on my muddy underwear. I peek back around my shoulder at Rahlan. My glance catches his attention, and I quickly look away. Granted the murky water hides my body, the thought of being naked in a bath with him still makes me nervous.

Taking a deep breath to relax, I pull off my muddy bra and underwear and drop them on the old dress. Done.

With my back to him, I scoop handfuls of warm water over my hair, cleaning it out.

"You're just going to pretend I'm not here?" he says.

"I'm nothing if not determined."

Scooping more water, I'm a little surprised that he didn't swim over and twist me around to face him.

"Is the water to your tastes?" he asks.

I haven't had a warm bath since I was a child – back when I could fit in the cooking pot. "How do they heat such a large pool?"

He points to a rectangular slit in the wall beside him.

I glide through the warm water to get a better look. It's a channel, guiding a thin stream into the bath.

"'Tis from a hot spring," he says.

I scan the pool until I spot the outlet. It's another channel in line with the water level. They must've carved crevices throughout this whole building, which couldn't have been cheap. This is a luxury only for their lords.

His hands land on my bare shoulders, making me jump.

"Hold your breath," he says. My face goes pale. He's going to dunk me under. What if he doesn't let me back up again?

"No," I whip around and jerk my shoulders loose.

His hands quickly retreat. "What are you doing?" He stares at me like I'm mad. "Your scalp's not clean."

I sink in the water, bringing it up to my chin. He's just after a little bit of mud I missed. "You won't hold me down, right?"

He appears puzzled. "You're not making sense."

His actions weren't malicious. I just hadn't had time to prepare myself. He wouldn't save me from an arrow just to drown me in a pool the next day. I suppose I do trust that he won't kill me... at least not for no reason.

I turn around again, facing my back to him. "I'm ready."

His hands rest on my shoulders. I bring my legs up, and he applies just enough pressure to dunk me under the surface.

His strong hands rub circles around my head. I would've thought the pressure would be uncomfortable, but it's oddly soothing.

Just a moment later, his hands snap to my sides, and he pulls me to the surface.

I almost thank him on instinct, but I hold my tongue. He's the one who had me pelted with mud in the first place.

I float over to the opposite side of the pool. Rubbing my head with my hands doesn't give the same soothing feeling.

A man's feet appear in front of me. I squeak and dip down until the water reaches my nose. I wasn't expecting other people.

The human man carries a goblet in each hand. "Lord Rahlan?" he asks.

Rahlan nods. The man places the goblets on the ledge just a foot away from me before leaving.

"Would you be so kind as to bring my drink?" Rahlan asks.

I take a goblet in each hand. One is filled with blood and the other with water. "Only because you asked politely," I say, hoping to reinforce the behavior.

He takes a sip from the blood goblet and sighs with satisfaction.

I gulp down the water goblet without taking a breath.

He wipes the line of blood off his lips after finishing his drink.

"You drink from a cup now?" I ask. Will this be the new norm?

"You haven't eaten in a while, and I've spent enough hours carrying you around."

"Or you've turned over a new leaf?" I ask, hopeful.

He smirks, and alarm bells ring in my head.

"Grawr!" He reaches for me with a fake roar, fangs on display.

I squeal and dive away. His hand grazes my foot, but I slide out of his grasp and pop up on the opposite side of the pool.

"Nothing's changed," he says, "That felt just as exhilarating as it always does."

His silly stunt makes me smile.

"Your gown awaits," he gestures with his head towards his clothes. "I'll purchase a more suitable outfit tomorrow."

I float over to the ledge and find a white linen nightgown folded beside his things. It looks about my size, but it sports a deep v neck that's not as modest as I'd prefer.

A silver sparkle catches my eye – his curved sword. It's wrapped up in his cape, just begging to be taken.

I shake my head at the thought. I don't think I'd have what it takes to beat him in combat, and he wouldn't take too kindly to having his own weapon drawn on him. Besides, I don't think I'd have it in me to maim someone.

My gaze falls back on the gown. The thought of having new clothes that fit properly makes me giddy. I'm about to climb out when I realize that he's watching. "Do you mind?"

He lays back in the water, letting his gaze drift to the ceiling. "How can a shy girl have such a sharp tongue?" he says.

I climb out of the bath and flick the water off. He's confusing shyness with self-respect.

I pull the gown over my head while keeping my back to him. My skin is not completely dry, but it feels better to be covered sooner.

Having the gown on reveals that the deep v neck is more than just a fashion choice. The base of my neck is left bare. The garment only just covers the edge of my shoulders, leaving my entire collarbone vulnerable to fangs. I wonder if all humans are forced to dress like this.

He steps out behind me, and I hurry to the doorway to stay out of his way. Should I leave the room to give him more privacy, or does he want to keep an eye on me? I stand awkwardly on the threshold with my back to him.

An arm wraps around my middle, and I jump. He squeezes me against his side. "Need I hold you the whole way back, or will you walk beside me?"

"I'll walk," I mumble.

He releases me, and we leave the bathhouse.

The soft gown hugs my thin frame. It does a decent job keeping the cold air out.

We turn the corner and stop at a small inn. An inn? Why not his home? Is he going to drop me off here? Is he that confident that I can't escape?

The building is joined to the homes on either side, like it's part of one giant structure. Its warm candles light up the street where we stand, almost as if it's inviting us in.

Rahlan opens the door. The small room is crammed with two dining tables on the left, a reception desk on the right, and a set of stairs in the middle.

He greets the innkeeper behind the desk, a vampire woman with sleek black hair. She doesn't look twice at me, as if humans are part of her everyday life.

Without another word to the woman, he nudges me to go ahead of him up the wooden stairs. With Jaclyn's inky scar in mind, I'm careful to stay out of the woman's bite range on the way past.

His key unlocks a room on the third floor. It overhangs both floors below and has a window overlooking the street. I'm immediately drawn to it, kneeling on the bed to get a look. Though the streets are empty at this time of night, peering out such a high window is very different to what I'm used to.

Rahlan closes the door and lights the fireplace.

His bag is waiting in the corner. I poke inside in search of an apple. My hands land on the cold metal eyeball flask, and I quickly drop it in disgust. I don't know why he has the need to collect his dead victim's eyes, and I'd prefer never to find out.

There's just one apple left. I quickly munch through it, but it's not nearly enough to fill the hole that's been growing for the last day and a half. It's too late to fetch food now, but hopefully we'll get some tomorrow.

A piece of paper catches my eye. It's the letter he took from the human men we encountered at the river. He doesn't seem to mind me digging through his stuff, so I pick the letter out of the bag.

I never learned to read, so the letter is not much more than a series of endless repeating symbols and scribbles to me. I was hoping for a map or diagram to decipher. One symbol stands out – the bow crest. This is a letter about the Huntsmen. Based on the way Rahlan was smiling when he read it, I'd bet it leads to Ivan, or at least he thinks it will.

My attention is drawn to another symbol. It looks almost like a styl-ized blacksmith anvil, different from the surrounding rushed scribbles. It doesn't ring any bells. I bet the content of the letter would explain it. I'm tempted to ask what the scribbles say, but I figure that it'll be better to appear oblivious about the Huntsmen and their dealings.

Rahlan unclips his cape, takes off his boots and hangs his coat on the door.

I grab the sleeping pouch from his bag and unroll it beside the fire. This cozy room is warm enough that I could curl up and just sleep on top of the pouch.

Rahlan pulls back the bed's duvet. "Climb in," he says, patting the sheet beside him.

I don't fancy sharing a bed with him.

"I'm happy here," I say from my spot on the floor.

"It was not a request."

I clench my jaw, and his eyes narrow.

At a slow pace, I make my way over to him and crawl under the blanket. He wraps his arm around my torso, and the feeling of his icy chest on my back makes me squeak. A human at that temperature would be dead.

I've slept up against him before, like when he kept me from falling from the tree, or carried me when the ravagers were on our tail, or when we were crammed into the narrow sleeping pouch, but this bed is more than big enough for the both of us to lay without bumping into each other. Why is he holding me?

"Can't I sleep in the cell instead?" I ask.

He lets out half a chuckle, then rests his nose on the crook of my neck and takes a deep breath.

"If you bite me, you'll be sorry," I warn.

"Oh, will I?" The smile is evident in his voice.

"I wet the bed when startled in my sleep."

"You're lying."

"Well you better be really sure," I say with a smirk.

His nose backs off, but his arm stays wrapped around my chest.

"You don't have to hold me. I've learned my lesson. I won't try slipping away," I say. Though I have every intention of getting away from this man, I won't try anything tonight.

"You are like a little fire," he says.

So the vampires want to syphon both my blood and my warmth. I sigh and wiggle around until I'm comfortable in his hold. At least the bed is cozy. Being a Lord, his bed at home must be even better.

"Why are we sleeping at an inn?" I ask.

"You prefer the wilderness?"

"Instead of your house?"

"I have no home in this city," he says.

"But we traveled so far?"

"This was the closest mounting city."

"Mounting city?"

"A gathering point for mounting the next offensive. I, and by extension you, have joined a campaign."

Chapter 16: Regiment

"Jacob!" I call, "Where'd you put the green beans?" The stew's almost done, and I can't find them anywhere. I know they're not his favorite, but he needs a balanced diet, and they're about to go off.

"Come on little sis, can't we skip the beans this time?" he says with a grin.

"That's what you said last time and the time before. Stop being childish."

"Okay, okay." He raises his hands. "They're behind you, top cupboard."

I try reach for them, but they're pushed right up against the back of the highest shelf. "Jacob!"

"Hmm?" He raises his brows, mocking me with his green and gold eyes.

"Give me the beans or you'll be sorry," I growl.

"Julia," he shakes his head.

"The beans."

"Julia."

My eyes shoot open, and I squint to focus on the figure standing over me. It's Rahlan. I'm wrapped in the messy duvet on the bed at the inn. My heart sinks as reality sets in. Cooking dinner with my brother was just a dream.

I sit up, leaving the blanket over my legs. Morning sunlight streams in through the window, but my body yearns to fall back into the bed's soft cushions. I slept like a baby... in the arms of my captor.

Rahlan draws his sword, and I rub the sleep out of my eyes.

He takes a seat on the wooden chair and grabs a sharpening stone off the desk.

"Who's Jacob?" he asks.

"No one." The less he knows about me and my family, the better. The last thing I need is to drop clues which would help him track me down after I escape.

Suspicion flashes across his features, but he quickly dismisses it. The one upside of him thinking so little of humans, with the exception of Ivan, is that he couldn't care less about the details of my life.

I nudge up against the window and peer out at the street three stories below. The vampires weave between one another, some carrying wood, full buckets and heavy sacks. I'd have thought they were humans were it not for their pale complexions and exotic maroon clothing.

Sparks fly off Rahlan's blade as he scrapes it over the stone. The thought that he's sharpening it for his next encounter with humans makes me uneasy.

My gaze drifts back to the street. It's odd watching the vampire's completing their daily chores. Up till now, I've only seen them in brothels or angry crowds, but here they look so ordinary.

I spot the occasional human – men and women being led by their vampire masters- no, their vampire captors. One human woman seems to move freely through the crowd. She must have some special privileges the others don't.

Rahlan opens the door and stands aside. "Are you coming?"

I slide out from under the blankets and approach, stretching my arms. "I'm guessing that framing it as a request is another formality?"

He slaps the small of my back, making me spring forward out the room. I whip around and glare daggers at him.

"You're catching on," He closes the door. "Now are you going to wobble down those stairs at a reasonable pace, or do you need further encouragement?"

"Asshole," I grumble.

His eyes narrow, and I hurry down the stairs before he gets near.

As I reach the ground floor, a delicious smell grabs my attention. There's a table covered with freshly baked bread, cheese and strawberries.

I'm drawn to it, my mouth watering. I haven't had a full meal in two days, and this marvelous food is taunting me. Such a variety of expensive pieces could only be for a nobleman. But vampires only eat meat. What would a human nobleman be doing in a city like this?

Rahlan converses with the innkeeper. I'm tempted to pinch a block of cheese but quickly swat the idea away. This city could have brutal repercussions for stealing, especially from someone wealthy enough to afford such a meal.

Rahlan collected apples for me before, so it's not like he intentionally wants me to go hungry. I stand behind him and wait for their conversation to end, worried that interrupting him may spoil his mood.

He finally turns away from the desk.

"Lord Rahlan?" I ask.

His gaze lands on me.

I hold one arm in the other, keeping my gaze on his chest. "Do you think..." I trail off. All my confidence just disappears when asking for food. It's admitting that I rely on him, and it's embarrassing to be so dependent.

I avert my eyes. "Do you think I could have something to eat?"

"I ordered a meal for you this morning. Is it not here?" he asks, his face puzzled.

He quickly scans the room. "There." He points at the table.

My mouth hangs open. I can't believe what I'm hearing. That luxury meal is for me?

"Thank you!" I blurt out without thinking.

Before he has a chance to change his mind, I rush over to the table and pop a block of cheese in my mouth. It's divine. The bread is next. It has a warm puffy texture, fresh out of the oven. I follow it up with more cheese and a sweet strawberry. It feels like I'm committing a crime wolfing down this delicious food so fast.

Rahlan takes a seat at the table, and it dawns on me that I've been stuffing my face while standing hunched over the platter like a poorly mannered party guest. I quickly sit and take another delicious block of cheese.

He pinches a block between his fingers and brings it to his nose to inspect. "You really love this stuff?"

"Mmhmm," I nod with my mouth full.

He plops it in his mouth, and his face twists up the moment he bites. His fist presses against his lips as he forces it down, and I cover my mouth laughing. His expression is priceless.

"'Tis spoiled milk," he says with his face still twisted up.

My laughing calms down into smaller giggles. I take another block of cheese with a smile to show my delight, and he scrunches up his nose.

Grabbing another piece of bread reveals a small tin hidden underneath. I pop it open and gasp at the sight – two biscuits. Biting one releases a sweet inner filling. Honey biscuits!

I can barely contain my excitement or my smile. I haven't had honey biscuits in years, and they're even sweeter than I remember. Each biscuit is no bigger than my palm, and the first one's gone in just four bites. It takes all my willpower not to devour the second one too.

I close the tin and place it on my lap. Jacob will be ecstatic when I bring him a honey biscuit. It may be small, but it's delicious – just like Mom used to make them.

A few minutes later, I'm licking my fingers having finished all the food. That must've been the highlight of my week.

Rahlan's stare wipes the smile off my face. He pushes back his chair and pats his lap. "My turn."

My eyes dart between his lap and his lips. They hide razor teeth that seem reserved just for me.

He clears his throat, and I quickly stand. My gaze is drawn to his huge arms, then the sword on his belt. I have to obey him. He's going to syphon my blood regardless of if I resist.

I sit on his lap, and his arms snake around my middle. He tucks my hair over my shoulder, exposing the crook of my neck.

His teeth poke my skin, and I suck in a breath. It doesn't hurt as much as it used to. Does that mean my body's getting used to it? No. Impossible. He must've changed his technique.

The innkeeper doesn't spare us a glance, like it's something she sees every day. This is a normal part of her life. I don't want this to be a normal part of mine, but it's happened so many times that I've already lost count.

The minutes pass, and soon my heart is pounding. He retracts his fangs and pinches the wound. That couldn't be over soon enough.

The bleeding stops. I try stand, but his arms tighten around my waist.

"Julia," he begins. I crane my neck to get a view of him. "You may find this difficult to believe, but a couple hours in the stocks is a rather light-handed punishment for trying to flee. If you attempt to escape again, 'tis likely that you will be captured by someone less kind."

"How thoughtful," I spit.

"Runaways are executed, and my plans require that you live, so such an event would be rather inconvenient."

Inconvenient. Good to know that my death would be nothing more than an inconvenience to him.

He pushes me off, and I shoot him a dirty look.

He heads out the door, and I follow onto the busy street clutching the small biscuit tin. Butterflies fill my stomach. This low-cut night-gown is only really appropriate for indoor use.

"Stay by my side, and pay attention this time," he says.

We head to the town center, passing the stage and pillory. It has no victim today, but it's still littered with mud and rotten food. The vampires go about their day, none even glancing in my direction. Maybe they don't recognize me without the mud.

We pass the stage and enter a shop. The ceiling is almost twice the height I expected, and the walls are lined with leather garments. Some are decorated with metal strips and others with fur. There's even a small collection of daggers in the corner.

"I wish to purchase a fitted suit of heavy hide armor," Rahlan says to the vampire shopkeeper.

The garments hung on the wall are thick, with many layers of leather sewn together. I want to reach out and feel their texture, but being a little human captive, I don't think I'm allowed.

Both sets of eyes land on me, and Rahlan signals to come closer.

I cautiously approach. What did I do?

The shopkeeper wraps a measuring tape around my middle, and I tense. It's especially nerve-racking when a vampire that's not Rahlan puts their hands on me. One of them is more than enough.

His tape wraps around my midriff, then my waist and my chest. He checks the length of my legs, my arms, and the width of my shoulders.

Satisfied with my measurements, the shopkeeper picks a pair of brown leather pants and tunic off the wall. He lays them out on a large table and draws his knife along the tunic's side. The tape is stretched out as he makes a series of marks along its edge, then the cut is sewn closed, with the material overlaid to make it smaller.

"You're buying me armor?" I whisper to Rahlan, puzzled.

"I stated that I prefer you alive, and today we embark on the campaign."

I gulp. "You're-you're riding with me into battle?" I didn't think he'd go so far as to drag me into the fray, especially against my own people.

The shopkeeper hands the finished items to Rahlan, who then drops them in my arms. All eyes are on me again, urging me to do something.

I grab a long linen offcut from the desk and slide into a little nook out of their view. Ditching the nightgown, I tear the linen in half and wrap it around myself to act as a crude bra and underwear.

The pants stick tight to my skin as I pull them up. They're composed of alternating layers of leather and wool. The tunic hugs my middle and is heavy on my shoulders, but it has an inner woolen lining to keep me snug.

I wobble back into their view, not yet used to the stiff pants.

"Perfect," Rahlan says.

"It's much heavier than yours?" I say confused, thinking back to the time I spent wearing his coat.

"You're softer than me. You need the extra protection."

"I bet I could protect myself even better with one of those." I point to the shelf stacked with knives.

He chuckles and hands me a pair of boots. They're large and heavy, reminding me of his own. I slip off my thin homemade shoes and step into them.

Rahlan pays the shopkeeper with a couple of the glass pieces from his bag, and we head back out to the street.

We pass many vampires and the occasional human slave. I keep my eyes peeled in hopes of spotting someone I know. Not that I'd wish this fate upon others, but a familiar face would make me feel less isolated in this foreign land.

We stop at a stable, and Rahlan inspects the horses on display. He ignores all but the destriers, horses bred for war. He settles on a stallion with a black coat, just like the one he owned before, except for its white feet.

He rests his hand on the bridge of the stallion's nose. It lets out a breath, making his high collar flutter.

"I'll take this one," Rahlan says to the stable master.

"He's fifteen Prymni," the stable master says.

Rahlan picks out the glass ornaments from his bag and hands them over. He leads the horse by the reins onto the street and straps his bag to its side. I'm grateful that I won't have to carry that thing anymore.

I slip the biscuit tin in his bag, and he gives me an odd look.

"I'm saving it for later," I say.

He climbs on the saddle, and I have to crane my neck back even further to meet his gaze. I don't know what Neil and his companions were thinking going up in arms against this man.

He offers me a hand. I take it, and he pulls me up on the horse. I'm seated right in front of him, imprisoned between his arms. He has no trouble seeing over my head.

My fingers lock around the edge of the saddle, and I watch the horse's huge muscles move as Rahlan steers it towards the city gate.

"What are you naming him?" I ask.

"I have yet to decide," he says.

"What about Mittens?"

He almost chokes at my suggestion.

"What? It's a cute name."

"Yes." He clears his throat.

We leave through the huge gate we entered just two days ago. Even on horseback, I don't even reach a quarter of the way to the top.

My body tenses at the sight outside the city. There's at least a hundred, no, two hundred vampires. Each of them is dressed in either leather or fur armor. They're tending to horses, loading supplies, and sharpening their swords. I've never seen so many of them in one place, and I don't like it.

Rahlan notices me stiffen. "Looking forward to reuniting with your friend?"

Chapter 17: The Campaign

We're traveling southwest, back into my country, with the goal of slaughtering more people no doubt. The army moves in one long line like a snake. There are around forty men on horseback, and the rest go by foot on either side of us. They've brought humans along too, at least thirty, to supply their endless need for blood.

It's odd being dressed as one of them. I hope the humans forced along with us don't think I'm a traitor, though the idea of a human enlisted in the vampire military is laughable.

"Ya' Lord Rahlan?" asks the ginger-haired soldier beside us. My eyes are drawn to the large axe on his belt. With his stout build, I bet he could cut a shield in half with that thing.

"Indeed, I am, Sir...?" Rahlan asks.

"Ohan," the soldier introduces himself. "So why don't ya' let me share your horse instead of the slave girl?"

Slave girl. That's what they think when they see me.

"She needs to stay clean of mud, unless you'd prefer to keep me warm in bed?" Rahlan says, earning a chuckle from the gray-haired vampire behind us.

"Well," Ohan taps his chubby chest, "I'm real soft, I'd say."

Two men on one horse would probably overburden the poor thing. "I don't think Mittens could handle the extra weight," I add.

Ohan's eyes narrow, and the others chuckle.

"Even the human can see it Ohan," the gray-haired vampire says, "You've let yourself go."

I meant the weight of two intimidatingly tall soldiers, but they move on before I have a chance to explain myself.

"Ya' wouldn't happen to be the same Lord Rahlan who spearheaded the battle of Aldon?" Ohan asks.

"I am."

"'Tis a pleasure to meet ya, sir," Ohan says. "But I'd wager I'd beat ya' one-on-one."

"Five Prymni?" Rahlan offers his hand to shake, and Ohan seals the deal.

"What kind of a name is Mittens? Did you mean to buy a cat and end up with a horse?" Ohan asks.

"His feet look like they're in white mittens," I say.

"He does not go by Mittens," Rahlan says.

"Then what's his name?" Ohan asks.

"'Tis..." he trails off, not yet having thought about it.

"Slippers fits too," I interject.

"The fearsome Lord Rahlan, and his mighty steed, Slippers," the grey-haired vampire says, followed by murmured chuckles from the others.

"Be silent," Rahlan says, ruffling my hair with one hand. "You're damaging my reputation."

"That's a chatty little human you caught there," the grey-haired one says.

"'Tis true. She's odd."

"I'm Julia," I introduce myself to stop them talking about me like I'm not here.

The grey-haired vampire raises an eyebrow before giving his name, "Theron."

We travel for hours without pause. For the first time since I've been taken, I'm heading towards my brother instead of away from him. When the chaos of battle hits, I'll slip away.

I lean back against Rahlan's chest. His iron arms on either side of me eliminate the risk of falling, and they ensure that other vampires stay a healthy distance away from my neck. It's like being encased in a protective cocoon.

* * * * * * * *

I awake to Rahlan stroking my arm. It's evening, and the line of men has compressed into one big clump.

"You awake?" he asks.

"Mmhmm," I nod with a yawn. I didn't mean to fall asleep, but these new clothes are warm and sport a thick layer of padding. Combined with Rahlan's morning drink, Mitten's rhythmic rocking was more than enough to put me under.

After making sure I'm awake enough to keep myself upright, Rahlan jumps off Mittens. He puts his hands under my arms and lifts me up off him, placing me on the wet grass.

He ties Mitten's halter to a tree and joins a nearby group of men in hoisting up a large tent. They're popping up all around us. We're in the dead center of the camp. I bet he chose the middle to make it harder for me to slip away unnoticed.

He looks like he's done this a thousand times before, whereas I'm standing here like a lost dog. Bulky vampires brush past me from every direction. I try stay small and out of their way. As ironic as it sounds, I'd feel a lot less anxious if there was a rope tying me in place, like Mittens. Not that having my movement restricted makes me feel better, but it's a clear signal to other vampires that I am where I'm supposed to be, and hence am to be left alone.

But on the other hand, a tether would make me appear subhuman, or subvampire in this case. The last thing I need is further reason for them to look down on me. I square my shoulders and harden my expression. I need to show that I belong here, in the middle of a vampire camp, unsupervised. This is the level of autonomy I'm used to.

"We bring fresh boar!" a vampire shouts at the edge of the camp. He's one of around twenty men carrying dead pigs like handbags. Hunting dogs stand proud by their sides. The camp cheers, no doubt hungry after a long day of walking.

Soon there are fires blazing, with the pigs roasting on spits. Breaking out of the fire's trance, I turn to find Rahlan missing.

I hurry over to the tent he was building. It's complete, and he's vanished.

I scan the camp. Tons of vampires, but where's my vampire? I wouldn't be so worried about being separated if I wasn't surrounded by a horde of blood sucking murderers.

A cape in my peripheral vision catches my attention. I hurry in that direction. "Lord Rahlan?" I call, but the caped figure doesn't respond. Getting closer reveals that this man has blonde hair, and his cape flaunts a gold pattern, different from Rahlan's maroon one. It's not him.

I should get back to Mittens.

But where is Mittens? It's dark, and there's so much activity around me that it feels like I'm the shortest person in this whole camp. I head back in the direction I came, but before I know it, I reach the edge of the camp. No Mittens. No Rahlan.

A menacing looking brown-haired vampire is staring in my direction. He approaches, his gaze locked on me. My stomach does a flip. I'm at the perimeter, at night, looking out like I'm trying to escape.

I spin around and bounce face-first off a hulking figure, falling flat on my butt.

"Julia?" the figure booms. It's Ohan.

"Where ya' going?" he tilts his head.

I gulp. He thinks I insulted him before.

"Ya' lost?"

My stomach does another summersault. I'm on my own, and I'm a slave in his eyes, in everyone's eyes. He could take revenge on me, and no one would lift a finger to stop him. There are no laws to protect me here.

"Don't be scared child. We'll find Rahlan in no time." He smiles and offers his hand.

I stay frozen, staring at his palm. He doesn't seem to be holding a grudge.

I cautiously take his hand, and he helps me to my feet. He pushes through the camp, keeping my hand encased in his rough fingers, almost pulling my arm out of its socket. What if it's an act? What if he's taking me somewhere private to kill me in secret?

My stomach twists up at the thought. I pull against his grip, digging my feet into the ground.

He doesn't even acknowledge my struggling, forcing me to follow him to the fires. The fires. He's going to burn my hand.

Chapter 18: Among the Prisoners

I thrash and flail and writhe in Ohan's grip. He releases my hand, causing me to lose my balance and hit the ground.

He stares at me like I'm a wild animal, and Rahlan appears beside him.

"Ya' little human got lost," Ohan says. "Not so chatty anymore."

"Lost?" Rahlan shoots me a look, as if I committed a crime.

I get back on my feet and dust the dirt off my sleeves. "You're the one who disappeared," I grumble.

"Oh, there she is chatten again," Ohan says. "She must've just missed her master, 'ey?"

"Must've," Rahlan smirks.

I glare at him.

Ohan becomes distracted by the roasted pork being taken off the fire. He heads to a table, leaving Rahlan and I to ourselves.

The meat catches Rahlan's attention too, seemingly causing him to forget about my supposed transgression. He grabs a portion and signals for me to follow him back to the tent.

He takes a seat on a rock, and I sit beside him. A large piece of meat is torn off and handed to me.

"Thanks," I say out of habit. It's twice the serving I'm used to. I take a bite of the salty pork, and a groan escapes my lips. It's good.

"'Tis rare to see you thankful."

"Sorry my bad, it won't happen again," I say between bites.

Right as I'm about to take another mouthful, he pinches the meat out of my hands.

I jump to my feet, but he holds it up out of my reach.

"Give it back," I whine, clawing at his arm.

He smirks, again.

"Please, give it back."

He lowers his arm, allowing me to grab onto the delicious meat. I try take it, but his grip stays tight.

"Don't you have something to say?" he teases.

I let out a sigh. "Thank you, I am grateful..." I say in the most monotone voice I can.

He releases his grip, the smirk still plastered on his face.

"I am grateful that you're so easily fooled," I finish the sentence.

He reaches for my food again, but I spring away. I was ready this time, and now I'm the one smirking.

His eyes narrow. "I'll get you for that one," he says.

I munch down on the pork, only returning to sit beside him once I'm full enough that I wouldn't mind if he snatched it away.

My eyes wander around the camp as I finish my food. The fires' warm glow illuminates the vampires, all eating and chatting together in small groups. It reminds me of the Harvest festival from home.

"Is this your everyday life?" I ask.

"As of recent. Why?" he says.

"It's very different... but also the same in some ways."

"Just wait until you see the dragon."

I choke on my food. "The what?"

"The dragon. We'll pass him tomorrow. Fire breathing, wings, the lot of it."

My mouth hangs open.

The corners of his lip twitch, like he's trying to keep a straight face.

"You're lying," I say.

"Possibly."

"Prick," I grumble, rubbing my eyes.

A yawn escapes me, and I rest my chin on my hands. My body's still recovering from the grueling traveling over the last two weeks.

"Sit here." He points to the grass by his feet.

"But my pants will get wet?"

"It won't be long."

I oblige and sit facing him.

He's hands snap to my ankles, and he hoists me up into the air. I squeal as my whole world flips upside down. He's carrying me by my boots.

"Rahlan, put me down!" I whisper-shout.

He ignores my plea, taking me towards a large tent. I have to tuck my arms in to keep them out of the dirt. My head swings left and right with his steps while long strands of grass tickle my face.

He lays me down on the sleeping pouch inside the tent, and I yank my feet away from him.

"Now who's foolish?" he teases.

I brush my hair out of my face. "Clearly me for trusting you."

He takes off his boots, and I do the same. Five other sleeping pouches lay in a row beside ours, but the tent's empty.

I crawl inside our pouch and snuggle up. My leather clothing is a bit stiff to sleep in, but I'm not comfortable being in my underwear with a thousand vampires around.

Rahlan slides in behind me and wraps his arms around my chest, hugging me tight to warm up.

"Goodnight," I say with another yawn.

"Rest well."

* * * * * * *

Rahlan shuffling out the pouch wakes me up. He stretches by the tent's curtains, the morning light illuminating his tall frame.

A hairy foot appears over my head, and I tense. It steps over me, a vampire heading out. Another two follow, narrowly avoiding my small figure.

It's way too early. I pull the pouch back up to my nose and shut my eyes. All the extra layers from my leather armor keep me toasty.

"The sun won't wait," Rahlan says.

I pretend to be too deep in sleep to hear him.

His hands dig into the pouch and latch onto my sides. I'm lifted up out of the warm nest and placed on his lap.

I yawn, rubbing the sleep out of my eyes.

His fangs poke into my neck, and the pinching pain jolts me awake. He starts drinking, and a stray trail of blood travels down my skin. I catch it with my finger, not wanting to mark my new outfit.

This is definitely the worst part of being a vampire's captive. A battle is the perfect place for me to slip away, but how many more drinks will I have to endure until then? I'm about to ask him when the fight will happen, but then I remember his mouth is full.

He pinches the wound, satisfied with the blood he's stolen.

After a minute, he nudges me off him and rises to his feet.

"When will we reach our destination?" I ask.

"Why?" he raises an eyebrow, suspicious of my question.

"Wouldn't you wonder if you were me?"

His lips make a thin line. "We will meet your people at tomorrow's evening."

His tone makes me feel uneasy, like I'm considered an enemy informant who has infiltrated their ranks.

The curtain falls behind him as he steps outside.

"Let's not forget that it was you and your people who dragged me into this war," I call out after him.

A breeze pushes the curtain open. He's gone. I'm not going to stay here like a glass of wine waiting for his return. I exit the tent and scan the camp, not yet sure of where I want to go.

Everything is visible now that it's daytime, and I can get an even better view by standing on the rock from last night.

A group of humans catch my eye. Their torn and dirty rags make them stick out from the rest of the camp.

I weave my way over to them, making sure to stay clear of any wandering vampires, though they seem pretty preoccupied with taking down their tents.

The closer I get, the further my heart sinks. The humans sit on the wet grass, chained to one another. They're a random mix of men and women of different sizes and ages. A few are still asleep, huddled together for warmth. They look pale and sickly.

Their gazes fall on me, and I spot a familiar face. It's Jaclyn, from the cells. "Jaclyn?"

"Julia," she smiles.

I kneel on the grass and embrace her. It catches her by surprise, but she returns my hug. Us humans need to be there for each other.

A thin chain connects her ankle to another woman's, and there's a fresh bite mark on her neck, just like the one hidden under my collar.

"How did you end up here?" I ask, "I haven't seen any vampire women around?"

"My mistress sold me to the regiment. She always hated my guts, but to be fair, the feeling was mutual." She shrugs. Her perpetual apathy bewilders me.

"Well I suppose then this is an improvement?"

She smiles. "I can tell you haven't been a pet for very long."

"I'm not a pet," I mumble.

"Humans dragged along to feed an army don't tend to live very long."

Her words make me frown.

She lays back on the grass with her hands under her head as if she's relaxing under the sun.

"Your master feeding you?" she asks.

My gaze drifts back to the boney group. They've probably been walked for miles with little-to-no food.

"Give me a minute." I rise to my feet and head back across the camp. The vampires seem to ignore me, but I'm still careful not to step too close.

I arrive at the smoldering fires. There's a burly vampire cutting up the leftover pork from last night's feast.

I stand opposite his table and hold my hands together to try appear respectful. "Um... excuse me, sir."

His gaze lands on me, and he rises to his full height, well above my head. I resist the urge to look at the huge meat cleaver still in his hand. His expression says that he's less than pleased that I interrupted him.

"You should be chained up, human."

Chapter 19: Sharing Blood

Butterflies fill my stomach. "My-my master sent me... to fetch him some pork." Though I hate the idea of calling Rahlan my master, it does make me appear like an obedient slave just following orders.

He glares at me.

"He's over there," I point at our tent, "I can take you to him if you desire, sir."

He doesn't move.

I remain frozen. I'm bluffing, but I'd rather be in trouble with Rahlan than this man.

He strikes his knife against the table, making me flinch.

"Then go on." He gestures at the large piece of meat he's just cut.

I cautiously reach to take the pork, keeping a close eye on his knife.

"Thank you, sir." I spin around and hurry towards the tent, eager to get out of that conversation as soon as possible.

Once I'm far enough to be sure he can't see me, I change direction and make a beeline back to the humans.

At the sight of the meat, Jaclyn's face shows the most expression I've ever seen from her. She's stunned, and maybe even a little excited. I've got enough pork for her and a few others. I try my best to keep the large portion close to my chest to hide it from the vampires. Feeding the prisoners clearly isn't one of their priorities, and I fear they may consider it a waste of food.

I take a seat on the grass and hand her the pork. She tears a piece off for herself and passes it to the girl beside her.

"I'm impressed." She takes a bite.

A man tears off a mouthful and passes the pork on. I appreciate that they're all sharing. Everyone will get at least a few bites.

"The vampires must like you," a scruffy girl says as she tears off her portion. She framed it as a harmless remark, but I understood the underlying message.

I pull the hem of my tunic up to my belly button, just long enough to let her get a glance at the stomach bruises left over from Rahlan's attack. "Not that much."

Though it may not appear so to them, this has been anything but a cakewalk. Rahlan's dragging me along because he thinks I'm his link to finding Ivan. I don't want to find out what he'll do to Ivan when he reaches him, or what he'll do to me when he learns that I'm Ivan's niece.

"Well you have my thanks, Julia." An older brunette woman says, "I'm Mathilda, but you can call me Mattie."

"You have all our thanks," a man says.

I smile, but my gaze falls to the grass. They're still chained up, treated like cattle. I wish I could do more. I wish I could get them out of this place, but I can't even manage that for myself.

The whole group stiffens. They quickly hide their food, slipping it in their shirts or behind their backs. I whip around and jump to my feet.

There's a hulking vampire just a foot away from me. He has black hair like Rahlan, with the same pale skin all vampires share. I sidestep around him, but his hand lands on my shoulder.

"I'm thirsty," he growls.

I pull my collar back to show Rahlan's recent bite mark. "I've already been drunk from today."

A blow hits my side, sending me tumbling over the grass. I groan, clamping my arms over my aching ribs.

Before I have a chance to regain my bearings, he forces me flat on my back and straddles me, keeping my body down with his weight.

"I don't recall asking, stupid human," he spits.

My fingers scratch against the dirt, trying to pull myself out from under him. He leans in close, homing in on my neck.

I can't get a proper grip on the loose ground. His weight compresses my middle, making the pain from the bruises flare up again. I gasp.

"Only my master can drink from me!" I blurt out in a desperate effort to get him to back off.

He ignores my warning, and his fingers pull back the tunic's collar, revealing my vulnerable skin. My body shivers at the feeling of his warm breath rolling over my neck.

I grab a fistful of loose dirt and shove it in his eyes. He whacks my hand away and pulls back with a groan.

A hard slap hits my cheek. I ignore the stinging pain and shovel another handful of soil into his face.

He shields his eyes with one hand and chokes me with the other. I grab his arm on instinct, but it's impossible to move.

He clamps down, cutting off my air completely. My fingers dig through the soil, desperately searching for something solid.

A stone is placed in my hand. Thank you, Jaclyn. The vampire is still trying to get the dirt out of his eyes. I swing the stone into the side of his head. He wails and falls off me. I can breathe again.

I scramble to my feet. A layer of dirt is caked onto my back from the pressure. The vampire groans on the ground with his hands on his head, and the humans stare at me with wide eyes. I take off, running as fast as I can towards our tent.

"You're dead!" the vampire screams. I look back to see he's already after me, seemingly uninjured. How can he just get up after a blow like that?

All eyes are on me, watching the spectacle unfold.

I reach the tent, but where's Rahlan!? I spin in a circle searching for him. There's a figure in a cape by Mittens. I sprint to him and crash into his back, almost knocking him over.

He whips around, but I grip onto his cape like I'm holding on for dear life. My breathing is heavy, and adrenalin is coursing through my veins.

"Hand over that human!" the vampire shouts. There's blood dripping down the side of his face, mixing with the grass and dirt stuck to his cheek, but he stands tall like the injury is nothing more than a scratch.

Rahlan rests his hand on my shoulder. My fingers remain clamped tight around the cape's fabric. I can't take on a vampire almost twice my size. Was I supposed to just lie there and let him suck me dry?

"Did my little human best you in combat?" Rahlan asks.

"I'm going to beat her until her insides are outside!"

"You will do no such thing." Rahlan pulls my hands off his cape and approaches the bleeding vampire. He's even taller than Rahlan.

"There's a score to settle!" the vampire shouts.

Other vampires begin to crowd around the scene, Ohan and Theron included.

"She is my property, so her actions are my responsibility." He pulls back his cape, revealing his sword. The bleeding vampire glances down at the blade on his own belt. "If there's a score to be settled, then we will make the square, and settle it," Rahlan says.

The vampire growls, but Rahlan remains unphased, waiting for an answer. It's almost like he's looking forward to it.

The vampire grabs the hilt of his sword but keeps it in its sheath. His once pale face is red with anger.

Rahlan doesn't move. Their gazes are locked on one another.

The vampire glances at the gathering crowd. They are forming a square around the two of them.

A hand rests on my shoulder, making me flinch, but I relax when I see it's just Ohan. He leads me away, and vampires fill our places to complete the square, with Rahlan and the angry vampire alone in the center.

"She'll get hers," the vampire grunts. With one last scorn, he turns away and slips between the crowd.

The group of vampires murmur to one another, disappointed that a dual ended before it began. They disperse, returning to taking down tents and packing up supplies.

Ohan follows them, leaving me alone with Mittens.

Rahlan's gaze lands on me, and his eyes run up and down my body. He pulls my collar back on either side to inspect my skin, then he lifts my arms and runs his fingers down my ribs.

"I'm fine," I say.

He steps back. "Would I be correct assuming it was self-defense?"

I nod.

He looks in the direction where the bleeding vampire hobbled off, then glances back at me.

Without further questioning, his attention returns to Mittens.

I stand beside him for safety, picking the grass out my long hair. "You know, I'd be even better at defending myself if I had a knife."

He chuckles. "Though I imagine the number of altercations would only increase."

After his bag is packed, he lifts me up by my hips and places me on Mittens. It's a little scary how easily he can carry me.

He climbs on the saddle, trapping me between his arms like before. The men stream off from the campsite in a thin line, and we continue traveling.

* * * * * * *

We trek through the forest, pausing for a short break by a river. It's refreshing to wash my face in the flowing water. I can't wait until I'm out of Rahlan's grasp and traveling on my own, then I'll be able to bathe in private whenever I find a stream.

I'm going to have so many stories to share with Jacob. Usually he's the one sharing tales from his journeys, but none of them top the extraordinary experiences I've had over the last two weeks.

Night falls, and the line of men gather into a group to setup camp. I'm lifted off Mittens and placed on the ground. The dry pine needles crack under my boots as I stretch my legs. Many of the men use the pine trees as a base for their tents. The lack of underbrush makes this an ideal place to camp.

"Hiding behind the trees!?" Ohan calls, "Did ya' chicken out!?"

Rahlan grins. He collects two wooden practice swords from a weapon bag and heads to meet Ohan.

"Too scared to fight with steel?" Ohan taunts. Theron follows with a smirk, enjoying Ohan's show.

Rahlan tosses Ohan a wooden sword. "I wouldn't want to injure you."

Ohan chuckles, waving the sword around to get a feel of it. Rahlan takes his stance with the wooden blade extended in front of him.

Ohan charges forward and swings in a wide arch. Their blades meet with a loud crack, echoing through the camp. Ohan yanks his blade away and thrusts it forward, aiming for Rahlan's stomach. Rahlan parries, sending the sword off to the side and leaving Ohan off balance. He whips his blade around, narrowly missing Ohan's overextended arm.

Rahlan's wooden sword is straight, unlike the curved blade he uses in real combat, and Ohan seems to prefer an axe. Despite the fact that they're both somewhat out of there element, their movements are quick and fluid with years of experience behind them. It looks frightening, but also a little fun.

Ohan swings for Rahlan's legs, but it's deflected. He doubles back and aims his return swing for the head. Rahlan ducks, dodging the sword and lunging forward with his own attack. The momentum of Ohan's failed swing stops him from reacting in time, and Rahlan's sword hits Ohan's chest. His thick tunic protects him from the wooden blade, but the force knocks him off his feet. If that was a real sword, it would have gone right through him.

He pushes himself to sit up and shakes the pine needles out of his hair. "Two Prymni, right?" he says.

Rahlan helps him up. "I believe it was five."

"I heard ten," Theron says from his post by the tree.

"Shut ya' yap," Ohan says. "Double or nothing?"

His wooden sword lies among the pine needles. I pick it up and run it through my fingers. It's littered with little nicks where their blades met. They were hitting hard.

"'Tis your money." Rahlan offers his hand to shake.

Ohan takes his hand. "Deal, but I'm carving myself an axe."

I test the wooden blade against my leather tunic. Satisfied that I'm protected, I take Ohan's place with my sword ready.

Rahlan raises an eyebrow. I raise the wooden blade, pointing it at him like he did earlier.

He takes his stance with one foot behind the other. I shout my battle cry and lunge at him to throw him off. I'm shorter than him, so I play to my strengths and swing my blade at his legs.

He deflects my strike before it even gets close. The hard impact resonates down the sword, making my hands ache. He swings his blade with a smirk, forcing me to jump upright and stumble back.

"Dominant hand on top," he says.

I look at my hands and quickly swap them around.

He shoots forward with his blade in line with my chest. I try spring back but end up falling on my butt.

"Feet apart." He takes a step back to give me a chance to recover.

I jump to my feet and strike at his middle. He parries my attack and counters with a swing for my head. I duck down like my life depends on it.

His blade passes well above me, and I lunge forward with my sword aimed at his chest, just as he did to Ohan.

He pivots left, staying out of my blade's path. I only have just enough time to pull back before he returns a strike.

"Fast learner," he says with a grin.

"You'll regret teaching her that," Theron says with his arms crossed.

My breathing is heavy, and sweat beads on my forehead. This is way more exhausting than I expected. I take a deep breath, readying myself, then I pull back and swing forward with my hardest strike yet.

He blocks it, and the impact knocks the sword out of my hand.

My blade falls to the ground, landing beside his feet in the pine needles.

"Gather around! Gather around!" a man shouts across the camp. Theron heads off, and Rahlan turns to get a view, facing his back to me.

I charge at him at full speed, slamming into him and knocking him off his feet. He hits the ground, and I land on top of him.

He pushes me off and gets up again. "You've really got to stop doing that."

I dust the dirt and pine needles off my pants. "But it's my best move."

All the vampires are drawn to one spot. Rahlan rests his hand on my shoulder and guides me towards the gathering.

We group up with the others, and he lightly presses on my shoulders, signaling for me to sit down. I sit with my legs crossed, and Rahlan takes a seat behind me.

We're in the front row, just a few feet from the bellowing man. His cape is patterned with gold stitches. It must have cost a fortune. He's the man I confused for Rahlan last night. He stands tall and proud with long blond hair, his flashy clothes and arrogant pose distinguishing him from the other vampires.

"That's Lord Soran. This is his campaign," Rahlan whispers into my ear, noticing my bewildered look.

So Rahlan is fighting as a soldier under this man. Is Lord Soran also after Uncle Ivan? I want to ask Rahlan, but I worry that mentioning Ivan will only reinforce his belief that I know him. Rahlan's only dragging me along because he thinks he can use me to find Ivan, and that knowledge alone makes me uncomfortable.

If this whole campaign was just about catching Ivan, then Lord Soran would've ordered the men to keep an eye on me, and that vampire wouldn't have attacked me this morning. I'm pretty sure everyone here thinks I'm nothing more than Rahlan's favorite drink.

Does Rahlan know where Ivan is hiding, or is he just hoping we'll stumble across him? He didn't know back when he was threatening the Huntsman by the river, but the way he said that I'll 'reunite with my friend' when we left the city sounded like he was certain.

A row of vampires wait behind Lord Soran. They're the hunters, standing with their dogs beside them. They caught boars for tonight's meal back when we passed the river.

"As I have told many of you," Lord Soran begins, "tomorrow we will descend upon the human stronghold."

The crowd claps and whistles behind me, excited for the battle, the same battle which will kill more of my countrymen. The vampires will fight for wealth and fame, but the humans will fight for their lives.

Soran scans the crowd. "But apparently tomorrow is too long, you whine to me!" He mimics a child's voice, earning a laugh from the crowd. "We're bored, you say! We want to fight, you say!" I hear Rahlan's deep chuckle behind me.

"Let it not be said that Soran leads a campaign of boredom!" he continues, "Since we shall meet new humans soon, I wager we can afford to lose a few!"

The crowd cheers.

What?

"Bring out tonight's entertainment!"

Six men reveal themselves from behind the trees, each holding a human woman. Their disgusting hands are locked around the women's arms. The crowd roars, and my stomach roils. They've got Jaclyn.

Chapter 20: Hunted

The six men line the women up to face the crowd, keeping their arms pinned behind their backs. Lord Soran struts between them, his gold-threaded cape sparkling from a fire nearby.

He pauses by Jaclyn, and she refuses to look up at him. Her eyes remain unfocused, gazing into the distance like she's miles away.

He twists her ragged shirt in his fist. The vampire behind her removes his hold, stepping back.

"As is most obvious, these weak creatures would not last long in a fight!" Soran shoves her back. She stumbles and hits the ground, drawing more chuckles from the crowd. These disgusting vampires and their lust for blood are the only reason she's weak.

The vampire behind her grabs her arms again and forces her upright. She keeps her eyes forward, avoiding the crowd and Soran.

"The way of the human is to run, not fight, so we shall let them run." He draws a dagger from his belt. "They will run for their lives."

He cups Jaclyn's chin, forcing her head up. "We aren't unreasonable," he says loud enough for the crowd to hear. "The humans will have a ten-minute head start."

Jaclyn doesn't react, her eyes glazed over. He releases her and circles back to the first woman.

I turn back to Rahlan with a pleading look. He's a lord too. Can't he end this?

His gaze stays focused on the show, ignoring me. He doesn't care.

Soran signals for the hunters to join him. Seven vampires present themselves to the crowd, each with a dog by their side.

"Which one of these men will be the first to return with a head in hand!?" Soran says. My stomach feels queasy. How can they talk about murder like it's a game?

Soran grabs the hand of a brown-haired vampire and raises it to the air. "Will it be Anker, the irritable!?" He grabs another one's hand, "Or Osald, the smelly!?"

The crowd laughs.

"Hans, the..." Soran's eyes run up and down the young man's frame as he tries to think of a title, "the lean." He continues through the hunters. "Jorn, the wrathful, Ove, the loony, Flote, the dirty, or Silas, the hungry? Place your wages!"

A noise erupts from the crowd, and the jingle of coins changing hands fills the air. These women are going to lose their lives for nothing but a night of gambling.

Soran signals the hunters with a flick of his hand. They pull the huge dogs towards the women, and their muscles tense as the dogs sniff their clothes. "This is the humans' chance to earn their freedom," Soran says, "Though I suspect none will be so fortunate."

He nods, and the vampires shove the women into the dirt.

"Nine minutes and fifty seconds!" Soran shouts.

The women scramble to their feet and stumble away on wobbly legs, the blood loss evident in their sluggish movements. The men cheer and the dogs bark. A hill stands in the way, making it even harder on their weakened bodies.

Jaclyn trips, and the crowd laughs. "No hurry sweetheart!" a vampire shouts. "Don't run too fast now! We'll be seeing that one soon."

How can they take pleasure in this? I shoot Rahlan a look of disgust, but he's not bothered. They're monsters, all of them.

Jaclyn and the others slip out of site over the ridge. They're so tired that their moving no faster than a brisk walk. The men rise to their feet, beaming with energy.

This is sick. They're people, human beings, forced to play the role of animals. They're going to die, and if that wasn't bad enough, the vampires turned it into a cruel game. Jaclyn is going to be slaughtered. I can't let that happen. I can't.

I run.

The crowd roars behind me. Neither Soran nor the hunters try stop me as I shoot past.

"We have a volunteer!" Soran says.

"Stop!" Rahlan shouts. I glance back at him before continuing up the hill. He's being held back by two hunters.

"She still has five minutes," Soran says.

Soon I'm over the short hill and the camp is out of sight. Thick pine trees block out the moonlight, darkening the forest. The women are nowhere to be seen, but I don't stop running.

"Jaclyn!" I shout. One vampire has drunk from me today, not eight. I should quickly catch up to her.

"Jaclyn! Jaclyn, where are you!?" I weave between the trees at full speed.

"Julia," I hear a soft voice behind me. My boots skid across the pine-needle covered ground, bringing me to a halt. Jaclyn's resting against a tree, barely able to keep herself upright.

I quickly prop her up on my shoulder.

"Why are you-" she stops. "What's the plan?"

They have dogs, and she can barely stand. We can't run. "We fight."

She smiles, letting out an exhausted breath. I guide her to a pair of trees with thick branchy trunks.

"We can't win," she says, "You should leave me. Escape."

"We don't have to win." I help her sit down, propping her up against the trunk so she's facing towards the camp. "We just have to stall."

I grab a heavy branch from a nearby fallen tree and climb up the trunk opposite hers. It takes all my strength to pull myself up while carrying the makeshift club.

Once I'm hidden in the tree's prickly needles, I take a deep breath and shout at the top of my lungs, "Rahlan!"

"Are you nuts!?" Jaclyn whisper-shouts.

I climb a little higher, submerging myself deep within the prickly needles. The tree trunk hides me from any approaching vampires, but it also blocks my view.

"See anyone?" I ask.

She shakes her head, looking defeated.

"When you escape these monsters, meet me at Fekby village, in Faria," I whisper. It's risky to share where I plan to go after I escape, but I trust her to hold her tongue, and I need her to believe that we'll get through this.

She keeps her gaze forward.

The forest is silent, bar the occasional cricket's chirp. I breathe through my mouth to be as quiet as possible.

"There's one," she whispers, "He sees me."

A dog barks, and I flinch. I resist the urge to look around the trunk. Any movement could give my position away.

Jaclyn begins shuffling around the tree, trying to put a barrier between herself and the hunter.

"Don't move," I whisper, "Draw him in."

"He has a bow."

"If he thinks you've given up, he'll draw it out."

Her lips make a thin line, unimpressed with my plan.

"Alf," the hunter commands, and the dog goes silent.

Jaclyn keeps her eyes forward. Looking up would alert the hunter to my presence.

My heart is racing again.

The hunter's footsteps crack the dried pine needles below me. I hold my breath.

"Pathetic," the hunter says in a scratchy voice. It's Anker, the irritable one. The dog barks again, it's teeth just an inch from Jaclyn's face.

My fingers tighten around the branch.

"Alf," he commands the dog again. Jaclyn remains frozen. Anker is too far away, just out of my range. Hold on a little longer.

He grabs her arm and yanks her forward. I stand in the tree. The dog notices my movement and starts barking. Crud.

Jaclyn is forced to the ground, and Anker's foot lands on her back. Ignoring his dog, he reaches down and twists her arms together, lowering his head. This is my chance.

I spring from the tree and slam the broken branch over his skull.

The dog goes wild, and Anker collapses on top of Jaclyn. She groans from the extra weight.

I raise the branch for a second strike, but the giant dog bites my calf, making me lose my balance.

I hit the ground. The ferocious dog lunges on top of me and goes for my neck. I block its sharp teeth with my arms. The leather armor protects my skin, transforming the vicious bite into nothing more than a strong grip.

I punch it in the face and shove it off my chest, but its sharp teeth remain embedded in my sleeve. It drags me over the dirt, away from the others.

Anker groans and Jaclyn shouts in pain. They're tumbling over each other. He's pulling on her hair, and she's hitting him with a stick. He's concussed and she's exhausted.

I push myself to stand up, but the growling dog pulls me back down. It weighs a ton. I slam my fist against its head, but it keeps dragging me backwards through the dirt.

Jaclyn wails. Anker is standing over her, kicking her in the stomach while holding his head. She lays curled up, defeated.

Anker's gaze lands on me, and he draws a short dagger from his belt. I try slide away from him, but the dog pins me in place with its unrelenting bite.

Blood runs down Anker's face, and his eyes seethe with hate. No. No. No. I kick and squirm, but the loose pine needles roll under my feet, and the dog's grip stays embedded in my arm.

Anker stumbles towards me, raising his blade up into the air.

My whole body tenses.

Anker freezes. A curved blade rests on his shoulder beside his neck, glowing in the moonlight.

"Call off your mutt," a deep voice orders. Rahlan.

Anker discreetly flips the dagger in his hand. Rahlan pulls his blade back, pressing the curved edge against Anker's throat, forming a trickle of blood.

"Ont," Anker commands, and the dog releases my sleeve.

I jump to my feet and stumble around the vampires to Jaclyn. Her nose is bleeding and she's holding her stomach.

"Move along," Rahlan growls.

Anker turns away, grumbling. Rahlan keeps his sword extended until both Anker and his dog are out of sight.

"Can you stand?" I whisper to Jaclyn.

She nods, and I help her up on shaky legs.

A sharp pressure around my neck yanks me off my feet. I'm choking. Rahlan's dragging me backwards by my tunic's collar. I can't breathe!

My fingers dig under the leather to try take the pressure off my throat. I can't stop coughing and gagging. My legs flail about in the dirt, desperately trying to regain my footing.

Jaclyn limps a few feet behind us with her arm around her stomach.

My boots finally find a grip on some harder clay. I try stand, but he pulls me back faster than I can walk. I stumble and fall again, still struggling to take a breath.

He finally releases his grip, and I fall flat on my back. I take deep breaths, not moving.

He positions his feet on either side of my head, and I scramble to sit up.

We're back in the camp, and he's glaring at me.

I glance up at the sword on his belt, then at his boots, then back at him.

My breathing is heavy. His hands curl up into fists, and my body stiffens.

He wouldn't beat me again. Would he?

Chapter 21: Dinner

"Get up," he growls.

I stand with shaky legs.

He grabs my hair and twists my head to the side, facing me towards the trees where Soran gave his speech. I immediately shut my eyes. The sight makes me want to vomit. There's a decapitated human head on a post, the wood colored red with blood.

"Do you wish to end up like that?" he spits.

I shake my head as best I can under his grip.

He releases me, and I step back, keeping my gaze at his feet.

He leans in. I try take another step away from him, but he grabs my wrist. My sleeve is pulled straight, showing the scratches where the dog bit. Its teeth didn't even pierce the first layer of leather.

His hands land on my hips, and he twists me around to see my back.

"I assumed you were simply unlucky this morning," he says, "but in reality it seems you feel obligated to throw your life away." He pulls my tunic straight, knocking the dirt and pine needles off in the process.

I'm spun back around to face him. He points to my feet. "Move from this spot, and you'll spend the rest of the journey bound to a log."

I nod, holding one arm in the other. I know what I did was dangerous, but I couldn't just watch Jaclyn die. Risking my life to save her, a human, is incomprehensible to him.

He walks off, and I wait until he's out of sight before gently rubbing my tender neck. I hope it doesn't bruise. It'll be like wearing a sign saying that strangulation is just a normal part of my life.

I glance around the camp, careful not to look in the direction of the post. My weight shifts from foot to foot, but I stay in place. Vampires work around me, setting up tents and moving supplies.

I want to check on Jaclyn, but I know Rahlan would be happy to follow through on his threat.

I sit down, keeping my boots in the exact same position. It feels odd sitting on my own as busy vampires walk around me.

A stocky man dumps a pile of wood in a ditch. It's Ohan. I'm glad to see one of the few friendly vampires.

I give him a small wave, and he chuckles. He taps Theron on the shoulder, and he smiles at the sight of me. I must look quite ridiculous with all these pine needles dirtying my blonde hair.

They lay down kindling and strike a fire. I watch them nurse the flame, absentmindedly picking the dirt and debris out of my hair.

My eyes wander around the camp. Many vampires are drinking from humans. I spot Jaclyn among the other prisoners, the ones who weren't selected to die. She made it back. Thank goodness.

A hunter emerges from the trees with a bag on his shoulders. The shape alone tells me exactly what's in it. The nearby vampires cheer, like this is some sort of victory.

The hunter takes a head out of the bag. I glance at the face for just a moment. I remember her. She smiled when taking a bite of the food I smuggled them. They took her home, her freedom, her blood, her dignity, and now her life.

The head is carried to a large group of vampires, blocking my view. Grunts and growls emanate from the group as money changes hands and debts are settled. These vampires are heartless.

I scan the group for Rahlan, looking for his distinct maroon cape. He's not there, which I'm grateful for.

"The flames ready?" Rahlan asks. I whip around. He's carrying a pig's leg leaking blood.

The image of the bloody head on the post jumps to the front of my mind. I press my fist against my mouth and rock in place.

"Perfect," Ohan says.

I keep my gaze on the dirt in front of me. Ohan and Theron take their seats around the small fire, and Rahlan sits beside me.

A new vampire steps into the circle, grabbing our attention. He hands Theron a small bag of coins before quickly disappearing again.

Theron begins funneling the coins into his own pouch, and Ohan shifts closer, "How much did ya' make?"

Theron ties his pouch closed and smirks. "None of your concern."

"Don't you owe-"

"I paid you off weeks ago, and I warned you against betting on Hans. He barely appears to have the strength to carry a head, let alone separate it from a body with the layers of tissue and-"

"Can you please talk about something else," I blurt out.

They pause. My eyes remain on my boots. I'm not trying to be fierce. I just want those images out of my head.

"Right, um, Julia" Theron begins, "I did not mean to scare you."

I hug my knees closer.

"So Rahlan, that's a peculiar sword ya' got there," Ohan says.

"I went through many before settling on her," Rahlan says.

"Wanted one to match the shape of ya' cock?"

They all laugh. It may be vulgar, but I'll take crude jokes over descriptions of human decapitation any day.

"So what does Lord Rahlan desire that he'd join our meager campaign? Fame? Riches? Slaves?" Theron asks. I feel like he glanced at me at the last suggestion.

Rahlan rests his chin on his hand, mulling it over. "Riches."

I look up at him, confused. He gives me a sidelong glance, silently warning me not to challenge him. Riches are the furthest thing from his mind.

Ohan hands him a chunk of pork. Rahlan takes a few bites, seeming to enjoy the taste.

His eyes land on me. "You hungry?"

I shake my head. My appetite disappeared the moment I saw the post.

"And what do you desire, Theron?" Rahlan asks.

Theron smiles. "Riches."

"And Ohan?"

"Fame," Ohan says, "Oh and slaves."

Rahlan raises an eyebrow.

"One slave. A cute one," Ohan says.

"I heard King Frode's assembling his army to the east," Theron says.

"Unlikely," Rahlan says, "he's a coward."

"Maybe, but a coward with many men."

"Humans are weak," Ohan says, "And I'm ready for a more challenging foe, wouldn't ya' agree?"

I don't know who they're talking about, and right now I'm too tired to be interested. I fought off a vampire trying to suck my blood this morning, and another one trying to kill my friend this evening. I'm exhausted. I've lost count of how many times I've been knocked off my feet today. If it wasn't for this armor, I'd be covered in bruises.

I want to sleep, but Rahlan threatened to tie me to a log if I moved from this spot. Does he expect me to sleep here until he's ready?

I yawn, waiting for a pause in the conversation before speaking up. "Lord Rahlan, may I go sleep?"

"Our tent is beside Mittens," he says.

"Mittens?" Theron smirks, earning a scowl from Rahlan.

I head towards the large tent, avoiding the other groups of less-friendly vampires. The further I go, the more it feels like they're watching me. It's dark, and soon Rahlan and the others are out of sight.

What if that vampire from this morning sees me?

I quicken my pace, stepping far from any trees or rocks which he could be hiding behind. I just need to make it to the tent, then I'll be safe. Just a little further.

I yank the tent curtain open. Three vampires inside instantly look at me.

I suck in a breath. Rahlan's sleeping pouch is just one of five. I back away, hiding behind the curtain.

I can't just sleep pretending those vampires don't exist. They could turn on me at any moment. And what if the vampire from this morning stumbles across me? What if Anker finds me?

I run back to Rahlan and the other two vampires I know. My boots skid to a stop just a few feet from him.

He looks up at me, raising an eyebrow.

"Will you please come to sleep?" I ask, trying to keep my voice low enough that the others can't hear.

"Later." He turns back to Theron. "He wouldn't go that far. His prince is wedded to one of our ladies."

I frown.

He continues his conversation with the others, losing me with names and places I don't know.

I sit beside him against the rock. The spike of adrenaline wears off, and soon I'm yawning again. I can hardly keep my eyes open.

Rahlan seems to notice. He puts his arm around me, letting me lean against his side.

Their murmuring conversation is almost like a lullaby, merging with the laughing and chatting around the camp.

My eyes close, and I snuggle up against him, resting my head on his side. I wonder if he's just feigning kindness in hopes that I'll turn against Ivan. It feels wrong to nuzzle up against a vampire, but I'm safer with him than any other place in this camp, at least for now, while he needs me.

Soon I'm crossing in and out of sleep, not sure which sounds I'm imagining and which are really there.

"Ya' human is adorable," Ohan says in a low voice. The word 'human' draws me back into their conversation.

Rahlan ever so gently strokes my side with his hand. "She has her moments."

"Where'd ya' get one like that?"

"She fled from a village I passed through. From the look on her face, I'd say I was the first vampire she'd laid eyes on."

The look on my face - he'd be terrified too if he was in my position.

Ohan chuckles, "Did she fight ya'?"

"She's no soldier," He draws a circle on my side, "but she did sing."

Ohan gawks. "She sang to you?"

"It was terrible. I think it's her weapon of choice."

Jerk.

"If a human sang to me, I'd do whatever they asked," Ohan says.

Rahlan sighs. "I gave in."

Ohan laughs again. "Did ya' pick her cause she's pretty?"

What?

"My choices were limited, but it didn't hurt," Rahlan says.

Rahlan thinks I, a human, am pretty? I thought he looked upon all humans with nothing but disdain.

"I think I'll grab one at tomorrow's battle. One like yours," Ohan says.

I'm not his.

Soon another wave of exhaustion washes over me, and I've lost track of their conversation again.

My thick clothes keep me warm and toasty, and though I don't want to admit it, Rahlan does make a good cushion.

* * * * * * *

I'm moving.

My eyes peek open. Rahlan's carrying me in his arms. I relax again. I'm safe. Well as safe as I can be in a vampire camp. I close my eyes and hug my chest to keep warm.

He takes my boots off, then he lays me down in the sleeping pouch before crawling inside behind me. His arms wrap around my chest. I let my body unwind, comfortable in the knowledge that those other vampires in the tent can't touch me.

A few moments later, his hands cover my nose, making it a little harder to get fresh air. I ignore it, too tired to move away.

The stale air begins to build up, becoming irritating enough to keep me awake.

"What are you doing?" I mumble, exhausted.

"Cold hands," he says.

I take hold of his wrists and tug them away from my face. I move them down into the sleeping bag and thread them under my tunic, resting his hands against my bare side. They're freezing. If it wasn't for his pulse, I'd think he was dead.

His icy fingers annoy my skin, but they'll warm up soon enough, and it's better than having my breathing obstructed.

This is my last night like this. My last night with Rahlan. Tomorrow we meet the human army, and that'll be the moment I'll escape.

Chapter 22: Jacob

"Julia, 'tis morning," Rahlan says behind my ear.

"Mmhmm." I nestle deeper into the sleeping pouch.

He inches me around until I'm facing his chest. "You are awake?" he asks.

I yawn and shake my head.

He nudges my body up so I'm at eye level with him.

"I want breakfast in bed," he says.

"Very funny," I mumble.

He pulls my tunic collar back and slides his teeth under my skin. I flinch from the initial sting, but my muscles relax once he stills.

My eyes close again, and I drift off as much as I can despite the dull pain. I must have a scar from having that wound reopened every day.

He finishes up, pinching the cut closed with his fingers. I'm awake, but I wouldn't mind spending a few more minutes in this cozy pouch.

"How did you scar your face?" he asks.

"What?" My heart drops for a second. Was I injured without knowing it?

He lifts his finger. "There," he gently touches the bridge of my nose. "'Tis like you were burned with many sparks."

I run my finger over the spot. "Nothing feels different."

He reaches for the sword above his head and unsheathes it just two inches. The reflective blade acts like a mirror. He touches a spot on my nose again. "There."

"Those are freckles," I laugh, "You had me worried."

"Freckles?" he asks, puzzled.

"You know, freckles."

He stares at me with a blank expression.

Taking a closer look at his face, I realize that he actually has no freckles. His skin is ghostly pale, broken only by his inky eyebrows and emerging stubble. I grab his hand and inspect it. Nothing. I tug his sleeve up and angle his forearm under the morning light, but there's not a single speck. "You really don't have freckles," I say mostly to myself.

He touches my nose again, running his fingers over it like he's feeling for texture.

He thought I'd been burned. The absurdity makes me smile. "Freckles are just little spots we're born with. It's just a normal part of being human."

He nods, his gaze still transfixed on my nose.

I stretch and pull myself out of the pouch. We slip our boots on, and I follow him out the tent.

The camp is packing up, and soon we're traveling again.

* * * * * * *

The sun is setting. Orange rays poke between the tall trees, illuminating the column of vampires.

The horse rider ahead of us twists around. I hope he's looking at Rahlan, not me.

"Twenty on south, pivot clockwise," the rider says.

What?

Rahlan repeats the phrase to the men behind us.

"What does that mean?" I ask Rahlan, looking up.

He pulls back on the reins, and Mittens comes to a halt with a grunt. His hands slip under my arms, and I'm placed on the ground before he jumps down himself.

He unties his bag from Mittens' saddle, dropping it on top of a small rock. The rest of the men do the same, removing bags from their horses and taking off their backpacks.

"It means you get to pick your favorite tree," he says.

I already know what he's going to do. "I don't like trees."

He reaches into his bag and pulls out the rope I'm all too familiar with. "Then I'm afraid you may find this a little awkward."

I step back, but his hand lands on my shoulder. He ties the rope around one wrist.

"You're an ass," I grumble.

"That hurt," he mocks, pushing my chest against a tree. The rope is wrapped around the trunk and attached to my other wrist, forcing me to hug it. There's no slack. I can't even sit down.

I glare at him as best I can as he climbs back on Mittens. He joins the other men. They move side-by-side, forming a front.

I wobble around the tree to try get a better angle.

The line stops advancing. I can only partially see the mass of vampires through the woods. They have their swords drawn. Is this the battle? It can't be. How could it just come out of nowhere? I can't spend the whole battle tied up!

I pull against the rope, but it does nothing but bite into my skin.

A loud roar cracks through the air. I stand on my toes to try see what's going on. They're charging. The horsemen are the first to go, quickly followed by the men on foot. Wherever Rahlan is, he's indistinguishable from the roaring mass.

I need to get out of here. This is supposed to be my chance. I can't climb the tree. There's no leverage. If only my one hand could reach the other, I could untie these damn knots.

I bend my arm around as much as the rope allows, inspecting the knot from different angles. There's a loop which seems to hold the whole thing together.

A distance scream echoes through the forest. I need to hurry. I bend a piece of bark so it juts from the tree trunk and try force it through the middle of the knot. The bark breaks, leaving it embedded in the rope without loosening it.

I angle another piece of bark for a second try, but the sound of horses' hooves makes me freeze. I peer around the tree. They're riding back. It's over already? This army of vampires traveled for three days for a five-minute battle?

Rahlan and the others return, reforming the column. He jumps off Mittens. There's no trace of blood, which I'm grateful for.

"Is the battle over?" I ask.

"That was no battle." He frees my wrist. "That was just a warmup."

I turn my back to him and untie my other wrist before he can see the piece of bark wedged in the knot.

He lifts me up and places me back on Mittens. His hand snakes around my middle as he takes his seat behind me.

I stiffen at the sight of a familiar face – Marcus. He's in line with a bunch of new humans being dragged into the column. They're bound together, with their arms behind their backs and blood running from various wounds.

Marcus's gaze locks with mine. He's just as shocked to see me. He's from my village, and he travels everywhere with Jacob. The idea being that two are safer than one. Why isn't he in Fekby with my brother now?

"Something wrong?" Rahlan asks. His hand rests on my abdomen, no doubt able to feel my tension.

"I'm fine," I quickly avert my eyes, not wanting to draw any attention to Marcus.

The line resumes its course. I discreetly peer around the column, trying to spot Marcus's brown hair, but he's being led too far ahead of us.

A heavy bell begins in the distance. Clang clong clang clong. It rings and rings, getting louder with every step we take.

The forest opens up to a clearing. There's a city – a human city. The bell rings in alarm from behind its yellow stone walls. Two large wooden doors creek closed, and screaming men and women sprint to slip through them before they seal. I don't blame them. I'd be terrified too.

Archers line the walls, and I start feeling a little anxious. Usually I'd wish nothing more than for a vampire army to be wiped out by humans, but I'm in the front lines among them, dressed in vampire leather armor. Any human will see me as a traitor, and the vampires would laugh at the idea of allying with a feeble human. I'm an enemy to both sides.

The archers don't fire, but they stand ready. The rest of the vampires pour out beside us, lining up at the edge of the clearing. They know exactly where to stop to stay out of range while remaining in the open, making their fearsome presence known.

"We'll be meeting your friend at dawn," Rahlan whispers in my ear.

I shiver. This is the last place I want to see Ivan. I hope he's far away, far from the horror the vampires will inflict on the poor people of this city.

I hop off the horse on my own accord. The vampires unpack their weapons – swords, axes and large oval shields. They tend to their horses, chop down trees and begin building fires.

I weave my way through the makeshift camp, leaving Rahlan to his own preparations. I need to find Marcus. There are vampires guarding the edges of the line, keeping a lookout over their flanks while also preventing me from straying too far.

I spot Marcus's chainmail armor. He's chained up with the other humans, and Jaclyn's cleaning his forehead with a rag.

"Marcus." I kneel in front of him. His head is bleeding, and he's clutching his stomach.

"J-Julia?" he coughs.

"What are you doing here?" I ask. "Why didn't you go with Jacob to Fekby?"

He reaches into his tunic pocket under his armor, and a painful groan escapes his lips. He pulls out a thin chain and drops it in my hands. A pendant – my brother's necklace – the iron bow Ivan gave him.

My heart stops. Jacob loves this thing. He wouldn't just trade it away.

"Why-why do you have this?" I stutter.

"I-" Marcus coughs again, "I took it."

"I don't understand," I frown.

"That vampire you ride with..." He lets out a breath.

"Lord Rahlan? What of him?" My hands are trembling.

"A month ago... On the first day of the invasion... he took Jacob's life."

No. I rise on wobbly legs, and my eyes well up. "No..." I step back. "He..." It's not true. I can't breathe.

I run back to Mittens, tears stinging my eyes. He can't be dead. He can't be. It's not true. He said he'd meet me at Fekby. We were going to- We were going to rebuild. How could- He's not a soldier. It's not true.

I slam into Mitten's side. It's not true. It's a lie. He's mistaken. I rip the bag open and throw out everything. It's not true. I can barely see through my blurry eyes. The sextant and waterskin fall by my feet. It's not true.

"What are you doing?" Rahlan growls behind me.

It's not true. I pull out the eyeball flask and rip it open. The strong chemical smell assaults my senses. I'm shaking like a leaf. It's not true. It's not true. It's not true. I tip the flask upside-down, sending its sickening contents into the dirt. The white spheres cluster below me. The flask falls out of my hands, and I fall to my knees. He-he's waiting for me in Fekby. I let out a sob. Rahlan's boots appear. I turn the eyes over.

Each one, each one must look at me. I turn the eyes with shaking hands. Blue. Brown. Brown. Blue. Brown. Golden green – Jacob's eyes. I let out a wail.

It's true. He's dead. I scream. I scream and scream and break into sobs. He's dead. He was murdered.

A hand lands on my shoulder. Rahlan. It was him. I stand up on wobbly legs and slam my fist into his chest. "You murdered him!"

He grabs my tunic – a warning.

"You're a monster!" I scream at the top of my lungs.

His brow twists up, and his free hand forms a fist. He hates it when I call him that. Good. He should hurt like I am hurting.

"You murdered him because you're a monster," I spit. "A sick monster. A cold-blooded monster. You belong in hell."

"Everyone in that flask got what they deserved!" he shouts, shaking me.

Got what they deserved?

I grab his sword from its belt and thrust it at his heart.

He shoves me away before the blade can make contact with his skin. A kick to my chest sends me flying. I lose my footing and fall on my back. He kicks the sword out of my hand, leaving a sharp pain in its place.

He grabs my tunic and drags me backwards through the dirt. I wail and scream and struggle against him. I can't see further than a few feet with my blurry vision. It hurts, but not my face or arms or chest or legs. It's deep in my core, like there's a knife twisting in my center.

He yanks my arms behind me and ties my wrists together. My back is shoved against a tree. He wraps a rope around my waist, binding me to the trunk.

"You think you can just do whatever you want," I choke out between my sobs. "But one day you'll pay, you'll be hunted and slaughtered like the monster you are."

He turns to leave, not looking back.

"I hope I get to see it!"

He disappears into the mass of vampires.

The rope forces me to sit and watch them. I wail and cry and writhe against my bindings. I hate this. I hate him. I hate all of them.

Pulling does nothing but hurt my wrists, and my anger dissolves back into sobs. He's dead. Jacob's dead.

This was all for nothing. Everyday I pushed forward with the knowledge that it would all be okay. I risked running from Rahlan at night, I jumped in the raging river, I pushed myself to walk on aching feet, all because I'd find Jacob again. We'd rebuild. He'd find a new farm for us. Everything would go back to normal.

How can he be gone? Life was just beginning. It's wrong. It took me years to get over Mom's death, but things were getting better. No matter what happened, we'd push through together. Now he's gone. He can't tell me stories anymore. He can't argue over dinner anymore. He can't hug me when I miss Mom anymore.

My throat hurts. I can't stop crying. I bet the vampires are watching, thinking pathetic slave girl. I wasn't a slave girl before. I was Julia. I was part of a family, even if there were only two of us. I was somebody.

What am I going to do now? I had everything planned out – escape, reach Jacob, find a farm. Now what? I have no home. I have no family. No one is looking for me. Everyone hates me. I'm nothing.

I'm alone.

Tears run down my face. I'm just a slave girl, Rahlan's slave girl. Cuddling in his arms, I let my guard down. I thought maybe he wasn't so bad. He lulled me into a false sense of security. I'm so stupid. I'm so stupid.

It hurts even worse because it's him. Why did it have to be him? Why couldn't he just stay home, with his wealth and his castle, stay away from us? He ruined everything.

Chapter 23: Ivan

It's first light. I didn't sleep, and I can't remember when I stopped crying.

The murderer is back, with his ginger-haired friend.

He kneels to my level. "Behave," he growls.

I spit at his face.

He grabs my hair and jerks my head forward, making my scalp burn. A gag is forced between my lips and wrapped around my head, pulling my cheeks back as it's tightened.

He unties my middle and loosens the rope around my wrists. I don't move, refusing to look him in the eye. I'm done cooperating.

He pulls my hands forward and binds them again, leaving a short length of rope so he can lead me and presumably keep my hands away from the gag.

The tension from the rope raises my bound arms and draws me to my feet.

I dig my heels into the ground and lean my body weight against him, providing as much resistance as possible. He yanks the rope, jerking me forward and almost toppling me over. I hate how easily he can overpower me.

I glare at their backs as they lead me deeper into the forest, away from the city.

A group of vampires are marching towards the gates. They stick in tight formation, using their huge shields to protect them from every angle. The human archers on the wall open fire. A couple lucky arrows get through, but the vampires just pull them out. They push forward, dragging a barrel on a rope behind them.

Rahlan and Ohan pull me further back behind the tree line before turning to circle the city.

I catch another glimpse of the vampires before the wall blocks my view. They reach the gates, and the human soldiers drop large rocks and steaming water from the walls. One hits a vampire directly on the head, and I shiver as he falls to the ground. His arms and legs are riddled with arrows. This is it – a warzone.

The three of us continue around the east side of the city, edging closer to the wall with the tree line. An archer up there would make short work of us – well at least of me, and that thought keeps my shoulders tense.

Rahlan passes my rope to Ohan. Ohan's hands clasp together, giving Rahlan a boost as he begins climbing a large tree. His maroon black cape flutters beneath him with every stride upward. The trees trunk stretches high into the sky, sprouting thick branches that nearly over-hang the city wall.

I look up at Ohan, and he meets my gaze with an apologetic expres-sion. He could just let me go. I raise my bound wrists to him, willing him to release me. My gag would turn any words into a humiliating mumble.

He shakes his head.

Rahlan positions himself high in the tree, still hidden behind the pine needles. A human stands guard on the wall with his back to us. His eyes are on the gate on the opposite side of the city. Rahlan nudges closer, not making a sound.

I need to alert the man before Rahlan takes his life. I take in a breath but hesitate before making a sound. What if the man whips around and sees me first? I'm beside a vampire, dressed in vampire leather armor. Those arrows in his quiver could end up embedded in me, like the vampires at the gate.

Rahlan moves into striking position. He's going to kill the man if I don't do something now.

I scream into the gag. A hand immediately slaps over my mouth, turning my scream into a squeak.

I look up at Ohan the best I can under his grip. He shakes his head again, and the guard remains oblivious to our presence.

A black plume of smoke rises into the sky. Something's burning at the city entrance. Human soldiers rush across the wall towards the gate, passing right over us, but the single guard remains at his post.

I stare at the back of his head wishing I could compel him to follow them.

Rahlan springs from the tree and lands on the wall. Ohan charges forward and the rope forces me to follow.

We reach the wall free of arrows. There's a shout, but it quickly becomes muffled. Something crashes to the ground just two feet away from me, and I nearly jump out of my skin. It's the guard in chainmail armor, dead from the fall. Another one of Rahlan's victims. It feels like I'm surrounded by death every day.

A rope is tossed over the side. Ohan secures it to the loop holding my wrists together. My eyes widen to the size of saucers at the thought of suffering the same fate as the guard.

"Don't worry." He pats my shoulder. "'Tis a good knot."

I hope so.

He tugs on the rope, and it's pulled upward, first raising my arms then my whole body off the ground. I groan from the stress on my shoulders. Ohan retreats back into the forest, and I'm hoisted up and onto the wall.

Rahlan begins untying Ohan's knot, but my wrists are left bound together. I glance at the sword on his belt.

We're on top of the high stone wall, and the walkway is barely wide enough for two people to pass each other. My gaze is drawn to the city and the myriad of thatch roofs. There are so many homes here. It's beautiful.

Rahlan jumps over me. Two swords clash from behind. A soldier has his blade locked with Rahlan's, and another soldier rushes towards me from the other side. I jump upright and shout to alert Rahlan, but it's muffled by the gag. There's nowhere to go. I'm trapped with a thirty-foot fall on either side of me. The soldier's sword comes flying down towards my head. I duck and use my arms as a shield.

The blade slices through my sleeve and cuts into my arm. I let out a wail in horror, but there's no immediate pain. Rahlan whips around and stabs the man in the shoulder through a gap in his chain mail mesh. The man screams, and Rahlan kicks him back, causing him to lose his balance and fall backwards off the wall.

Both soldiers are dead, leaving just Rahlan and myself.

The second it feels like I can breathe again, a sharp pain shoots up my arm and into my chest. I'm bleeding.

Rahlan grabs my arm and inspects the wound.

"You'll live," he says.

He attaches the loop connecting my wrist together to his belt and hurries across the wall. My hands are yanked forward behind him, and the sudden tension over the wound brings an intense pain. I scream.

He stops, turning back to him. My legs buckle, and I wail into the gag. My arm is dripping blood.

He unties my rope from his belt, finally realizing his mistake.

"Follow," he orders.

I shoot him a dirty look and wince from the pain again.

He heads for a guard tower, and I follow out of fear of the alternative. A young guard boy inside bolts the moment he sees us. "They're inside! They're inside!" he screams at the top of his lungs.

We hurry down the tower's steps to ground level. We're inside the city, and my arm is throbbing, but I'm relieved to be off that high wall.

He glances at me as a silent reminder to follow, and I glare back at him.

We hurry down the alleys between houses, crisscrossing from one street to the next. He's searching for something. I manage to yank the gag off my head despite my stinging wound.

We turn a corner, and he jerks backwards, pulling me with him. His hand smacks over my mouth, forcing me to stand flat against the wall beside him. Numerous metal footsteps hurry down the adjacent street.

He waits for them to pass before shooting around the corner. I take the opportunity to run in the opposite direction, back down the street we came. I will not be a part of this any longer.

I'm not even halfway down the road when Rahlan's arms wrap around my waist. He hoists me up into the air and carries me like a handbag, my body jerking from left to right with each step.

Turning a corner puts even more stress on my middle. Eventually he lets go, and I land on all fours on the dusty ground, the impact making my arm flare up.

He grabs the back of my tunic, and the pressure around my chest pulls me upright again. His hands catch mine, and he begins untying the rope holding my wrists together.

Houses are packed tight on either side of us. My eyes are drawn to the tavern at the end of the road. It proudly displays a metal plaque bearing the image of a blacksmith anvil. It's the same stylized anvil from the letter Rahlan stole from the huntsmen by the river. This is the place he's been looking for.

He finishes with the rope, freeing my wrists.

"Do you wish to live?" he asks.

"What?"

"Do you wish to live!?"

I flinch. "Yes."

He points to the tavern door. "Then you will go in there. If you see Ivan, you will return to me and point him out. If not, you will have someone there lead you to whatever little escape tunnel he's scurried off to. Understand?"

His red eyes are burning. I've never seen him so unhinged. The Rahlan I've known for the last few weeks is gone. No, he was never real. I feel like I'm a citizen of this city seeing a vampire for the first time.

He grabs my good arm and shakes me. "Understand!?"

I quickly nod.

He steps back, allowing me to move past him. "You have one minute."

I press the tavern door open and slip inside, quickly closing it behind me. It takes a second for my vision to adjust to the dark room.

Twenty pairs of eyes are watching me. Men and women sit scattered around the tables with drinks in hand, and a woman behind the bar is packing glasses into a crate.

Their initial surprise quickly fades. Figuring I'm just another citizen, they return to their drinks, murmuring to one another. I scan their faces. Ivan's not here. Thank goodness.

Rahlan expects me to figure out where he went, but I will not hand over the last member of my family to be at his mercy.

But what about these people? He could burst in here and murder one person after another.

What can I do? There's thirty seconds left.

"Listen, everyone!" I shout. Their eyes land on me. "You need to get out of here. There's a vampire outside, and he-"

The door screams open and crashes against the wall. Rahlan storms in, his face obscured by the bright sunlight. He grabs me, and my tunic tightens as his hand twists the leather by my back. His grip forces me up to my toes. The men and women shoot up, grabbing swords, kitchen knives and chairs as makeshift weapons.

A cold metal blade presses up against my neck – Rahlan's curved sword.

"Stay where you are!" he shouts. He's deranged.

The men and women shuffle around each other, the unarmed ones moving to the back of the pack. Rahlan's grip tightens, making my shoulders curl back. He angles his back to the wall, and his blade presses against my neck, forcing my head up. I take short sharp breaths, afraid he'll push the blade higher.

"This girl is one of Ivan's." Rahlan kicks the door closed, darkening the room again. "If he wants her alive, he'll crawl out his hole and take her. Tell him!"

If-if he wants me alive? No. No. No. My whole body begins to tremble. I can't die here. I can't.

"Hogwash," a man says, "If Ivan left without her, then she chose to stay like the rest of us."

"She goes by Julia – a good friend of Ivan's, and he would very much like her alive." He shakes me. "Tell them."

No, I can't. I can't tell them I'm Ivan's niece. If he comes back for me, Rahlan could kill him. How could I sleep at night knowing that I sacrificed him for my own life? I couldn't. No one will die because of me.

"Tell them!" Rahlan shouts.

I gulp and shut my eyes.

He swings me around and slams my back against a table. My head hits the wood, and pain radiates through my skull from the impact.

"Do you not understand!?" Rahlan shouts, glaring down at me. He presses his blade in the middle of my chest, pinning me flat against the table. "Do you not think I will kill you!? This is your only purpose! You are worthless if you can't draw Ivan out!"

He's ready to take my life. I'm going to die at his hand, just like Jacob. Jacob – I'm going to see Jacob again. Tears sting the corners of my eyes. I'm going to see Mom and Dad.

Rahlan angles his arm to be ready to drive the blade through me. The tip pokes through the leather tunic and marks my skin with a shallow cut. I wince and grit my teeth. "This is your last chance! Tell them how you know him, or you will bleed out on this table, and I will find him without you!"

I stare at his blade, blinking back tears. I remember the night Mom died. It felt so unfair at the time. I couldn't understand why she had to go so soon. One day I was screaming at Jacob from my own pain, and he reminded me that we don't remember Mom for her death but for her life.

Taking a breath makes me wince, the expansion of my chest pressing against the blade.

I will celebrate my life too, not mourn its end. I'm grateful that I had eighteen years, I'm grateful for the petty arguments Jacob and I used to have at dinner, and I'm grateful that I did not die in that shoddy barn when I probably should have. I had an extra two weeks. Though they were hard at times, I ate some amazing food, I enjoyed a warm bath, and I met a brave woman.

My blurry gaze meets Rahlan's again. I take in a pained breath. Tears flow freely down my cheeks now. There's no need for a tough facade anymore. It doesn't matter what he thinks of me. "Goodbye, Rahlan."

He grits his teeth, his arm shaking, making the sword ripple. I wonder if this was always his plan for me. When I slept beside him in ignorance, did he know that one day he'd run me through with a blade?

I close my eyes. I did my best.

"Bloody hell!" he shouts. The blade's pressure disappears, and his hand slams into the table.

I jump upright, and Rahlan charges towards the men. They parry his storm of frenzied strikes. The door bursts open, and two new vampires storm inside.

I duck under the table. The vampires rush to Rahlan's side, forcing the humans back. One man is cut down with a scream, and more of them funnel out the back.

Their backs are to me. This is my chance. I can get away! I bolt out the door we came through.

The city is breached. Screaming, fire and vampires everywhere. A horde charges in my direction. I run, skidding around a corner.

A blunt object strikes my head.

The sun is bright, overwhelming. I'm on the ground. Who hit me?

I don't know. My vision can't focus. Everything hurts. My limbs aren't listening. There's a loud ringing in my ears and a warm liquid running over my neck.

My eyes close.

Chapter 24: Trading a Lie for a Life

My eyes peek open, and a seething headache follows. I shut them again, hissing from the pain. My limbs remain still, waiting for the wave to pass.

I open my eyes again. It's dark. Night already? Was I left in the street?

No. There's a tarp overhead – a tent. I recognize the black and brown circular weave. This is a vampire tent.

I grit my teeth and force myself to sit upright, further aggravating the throbbing in my head.

I'm alone in this small place. The blanket falls onto my legs, and the air's cold embrace makes me shiver.

I'm topless. My stomach flips. Both my bra and tunic are gone, but my chest is wrapped in bandages. I yank back the blanket, relieved to see that my armored pants are still in place.

Tight bandages cover my right forearm, protecting the wound I got on the wall. The bandage around my chest covers the small cut from Rahlan's blade. I gently touch the sore spot on my head – another bandage. A vampire tended to my wounds.

My eyes are drawn to the thin curtain blocking the bright world outside. It wasn't some random vampire, Rahlan tended to my wounds.

I sigh and rest my head in my hands. He couldn't bring himself to kill me, but he's still hunting Ivan like a rabid dog.

The occasional murmuring makes it to my ears. The battle must be over for it to be this quiet.

Something pokes me as I adjust my leg. I pull the offending object out of my pocket. It's Jacob's iron bow necklace – the symbol of the Huntsmen. I wish he was here. He'd know what to do. My fist tightens around the necklace. If Rahlan saw it, he wouldn't be pleased.

To my headache's displeasure, I twist around and leopard crawl under the back of the tent where the cloth meets the dirt, peeking my face out from under the material before going further.

Ominous black smoke rises from behind the city walls. A large number of frightened humans huddle together on the ground, surrounded by vampires. There are wagons filled with silver, ornaments and—I cringe. Human bodies.

They are stacked high on top of each other with their heads hanging over the edge. I count four wagons of bodies, all human from what I can tell.

I squeeze the pendent in my hand, and an idea pops into my head.

A boot lands in front of my face, and my heart jumps.

The vampire moves on, not noticing me. I peek out a little further. A couple vampire's idle around the loot carts, but the ones with bodies appear unguarded.

I crawl out from under the tent and slowly rise to my feet. The pain lingers in the back of my head, like it's waiting for me to lower my guard before it strikes.

I take a step, but my feet slip beneath me, and I fall against a large wooden desk. A stack of metal swords on the desk slip over each other with a clank, and I duck at the loud noise.

A minute passes, and no vampires come to drag me across the camp. I step forward again, using a series of trees and stolen furniture to keep my balance. The headache creeps forward, but I stumble onwards.

The pain threatens to overwhelm me by the time I finally reach my target – the wagon of cadavers. Either none of the vampires have spotted me or they just don't care.

My fingers snap to my nose at the putrid smell. I scan the bodies, looking for someone with a slender face and graying black hair, someone who looks like Ivan.

I settle on a man who's little chubbier than Ivan, but he may be close enough to fool someone who's never seen him before.

I kiss Jacob's iron pendant goodbye and place it around the man's neck. Jacob would never take this thing off, even when washing in the stream. He was proud. I'm sorry, Jacob.

The necklace dangles out the cart, clearly visible to anyone walking past.

I turn and wobble back towards the tent. A wave of pain follows, forcing me to crouch and grip my hair.

My head is spinning. I'm on all fours, crawling back. I have to get back-

* * * * * * *

My eyes open again, and I'm greeted by the same black and brown circular weave of the tent.

"Did you rest well?" Rahlan's voice makes me flinch. I jump upright and blink until my vision focuses.

He moves closer and reaches for me.

I shuffle away from him and curl my knees to my chest. He held a sword to my throat. I thought I was finished.

He nudges forward again. "There is no danger."

My head touches the back of the tent, and the hairs on my neck stand straight. I still, trying to keep my hands from shaking.

He wouldn't bandage me up just to hurt me again. He wouldn't bandage me up just to hurt me again.

His arms wrap around me, and my body goes stiff. He holds me close to his chest and carries me out the tent. I grip his shirt in my fists. His arms are careful not to apply too much pressure, but firm enough that I won't fall.

A sharp pain in my head makes me wince. I lean against his chest to take the pressure off my neck, not caring what he or anyone else thinks. My body needs rest.

"Look," he says.

I glance ahead and immediately feel like throwing up. There's a line of decapitated human heads laid out on the table. I count ten, one of which being the bloodied head of the graying black haired man with whom I planted Jacob's necklace.

"Recognize anyone?" Rahlan asks.

The necklace is gone, forever. Jacob's most precious possession, the last piece I had to remember him by.

I point at the graying black haired man, "Ivan."

"Good girl," he says, the smile evident in his voice.

Condescending ass.

He takes me back to the tent and lays me down on the blankets. "Rest now."

I curl up after he leaves. As much as I wish I could, I'm in no state to run away.

* * * * * * *

I awake to the sound of wheels riding over gravel, the vibrations reverberating through my body. Clouds cover up the sun. I'm on a wagon.

A wagon? He sold me!

I scramble to sit up. An arm hits my chest, pressing me down. I writhe and kick against the man's pin, aggravating my head further.

"Be still," a voice commands – Rahlan.

I freeze, taking deep breaths. It's not over.

His arm disappears, and he takes a seat beside my head. I lay still on the blankets, my gaze locked on his towering figure.

He hands me the waterskin. "Movement will slow the healing."

I don't see why he cares.

Sipping the water, I slowly twist my head and glance around. The wagon is moving despite the empty driver's bench. We're alone on a road surrounded by grassy hills. Mittens draws our wagon, heading down the dirt road without Rahlan's guidance.

"He's a witty horse," Rahlan says, "Now rest."

I lay my head down on the soft material again. Rahlan hands me a pouch and returns to the driver's bench behind me.

I peer inside the pouch. Freshly picked apples.

I pull the blanket back over my chest and try make myself comfortable. The tall trees of the pine forest grow smaller and smaller behind us.

A hand touches my hair, slowly twirling the locks by my ears. I take another bite of the apple. It's just easier not to argue right now.

Four apples fill me up, but my headache lingers. I turn to my side and shut my eyes again. His fingers follow, carefully combing my hair.

We ride the road for hours, and the sun creeps closer to the horizon.

As far as Rahlan's concerned, Ivan's dead, so why slow himself down with a wagon just for me? Does he suspect that I lied?

I take another sip of water. "Can we stop for a moment?" I ask.

He obliges. "What is it?"

I push the blanket aside and slowly sit up. "Private matter."

His hands slip under me before I can react. He lifts me up and takes a gentle step off the wagon. The road is empty as far as I can see.

"Where are we headed?" I ask.

"East."

What kind of an answer is that?

He places me behind a tree and waits on the opposite side of the wagon.

I finish up and slowly stand, propping myself up on the tree.

He returns and carries me with a hug back to the wagon. I latch onto the wooden side and prop myself up as he places me back on the blankets.

His bag is just close enough for me to reach. I peel back the flap and peer inside. A shiny metal surface at the bottom of the bag reflects the dim sunlight back at me.

"Rahlan," I begin. His gaze lands on me. "I want to bury my brother."

Chapter 25: Healing

He averts his eyes.

I take the flask out of the bag and pull at the lid.

His hand lands on mine. "Let me," he says.

I glance down at the flask and hand it to him.

He opens the lid, and strong fumes fill the air. He places a strip of linen over the top, then flips it upside-down, allowing the chemicals to drain into another jug.

After the liquid stops, he lays out a second strip of linen on the wooden driver's bench. He turns his back to me, blocking my view with his torso.

"What do they look like?" he asks.

I swallow a lump in my throat, thinking of Jacob's beautiful eyes. They were special, unique, like him. I'm never going to see his smug stare again.

"Green and gold," I say.

The liquid is poured back in the flask, and he places a piece of folded linen in my hands

I peel back the linen and quickly cover them again.

He grabs a shovel off the side of the wagon and scoops me up in his arms. I keep the last piece of Jacob protected in my hands.

Rahlan hikes up a large hill, carrying both me and the shovel. He stops at the very top and places me on the green grass.

His shovel pierces the dirt at the highest point on the hill. He looks at me, waiting for confirmation.

I nod, and he begins digging.

My eyes wander around the open landscape – green hills dotted with red and white flowers. This place is beautiful. Jacob would've loved it.

Rahlan steps on the back of the shovel, forcing it deeper into the dirt. Another clump of soil is flung onto the growing heap beside him. The hole is already a few feet deep.

I slowly rise to my feet, careful not to agitate my head.

He strikes the ground again, ripping out a chunk of dirt and roots. His shovel stabs the soil without pausing, drilling deeper into the earth.

"That's fine," I say.

He forces the shovel another layer deeper with the help of his foot, not hearing me.

"Rahlan?"

He grits his teeth and flings up another clump of dirt. The shovel is driven down again, cutting into the ground and deepening the hole.

I step forward and touch his back. He swings around to face me, his breathing heavy.

"That's fine," I say again.

He steps back. I kneel down and place the folded linen at the bottom of the hole. My eyes linger on the small piece of white material. Goodbye, Jacob.

Rahlan waits for me to stand before filling in the hole. The dirt is flattened to match the surrounding earth, leaving nothing but the lack of grass as an indication of the grave.

He drops the shovel and heads down the hill. A minute later he returns with two large round stones in each hand. They're placed beside one another over the grave.

His figure disappears behind the hill again. I find a similar stone nearby, but it's too heavy to lift, so I roll it towards the grave.

By the time I reach the site, my arms are exhausted, and my head is aching. Rahlan has placed thirteen stones over Jacob's remains, forming a two-layer square pyramid. I try lift the final rock for the tip, but it just rolls out my hands.

Rahlan takes the final stone and places it on top, completing the small tower.

He takes a step back, giving me space.

The sunset tints the hills yellow. It reminds me of the plains to the north of our village. We found a cave and built a base there as kids. I wish I could forget everything, all of it.

I glance back at Rahlan, and he carries me back to the wagon. He tuts Mittens forward, and I lay back on the blankets, my gaze on the stone tower growing smaller behind us.

* * * * * * *

The stars are scattered across the evening sky. I rub the sleep out of my eyes. The slow grind of the wagon wheels is gone. When did we stop?

I sit up to stretch, but the scene around me immediately makes me shrink back down. Vampires. Everywhere.

I pull the blanket over my head like a hood and peek out over the wagon's side. I'm in the middle of a vampire camp even larger than the last one, and Rahlan is nowhere to be seen. Soldiers in red and gray armor stand beside large tents of matching colors, any of whom would be happy to slaughter me if I misstep.

Running would get me killed. I scan the camp for Rahlan. A figure wearing a familiar red and black cape steps inside an extravagant tent guarded by two vampires.

What's he doing here? What's so terrible that he wanted to keep me in the dark about this place? My stomach sinks. He doesn't need me anymore. He's going to sell me to these soldiers.

I climb down the side of the wagon, careful not to agitate my headache. My short uneven steps lead me towards the tent. This can't happen. I need to convince him to change his mind.

The chilly air nips at my exposed skin. I've still got my leather pants, but the tunic is gone, and the only thing covering my top is a wrapping of bandages around my ribs. I hug my arms over my bare stomach to try keep warm.

Humans don't walk around chainless in a vampire camp. Some are watching me, but I keep my gaze forward. The jagged motion aggravates the dull pain throughout my skull.

I rub my forehead trying to numb the ache and focus on my feet. Just a little further. Two guards stand on either side of the tent. Maybe they'll let me pass. It's not like I resemble anything close to a threat in my current state.

"Halt." The guard's gloved hand wraps around my bandaged arm and squeezes tight.

I let out a cry and curl back from the sudden pain that wasn't there before.

The other guard slaps the one holding me. "She's injured, numbskull."

To my relief, he lets go. Without taking a second to think about it, I dive through the curtain between them and land inside the tent on my hands and knees.

The impact ripples up my stinging arm and into my head. I raise my gaze, resisting the urge to close my eyes from the headache.

Rahlan is staring at me in horror. My eyes are drawn to the man behind him. He has a long face, curly brown hair and a silver ring on his head that glows in the candlelight.

Two iron hands lock around my biceps and pull me to my feet. "My deepest apologies, King Groel," a guard says, "We did not foresee her second attempt."

His red eyes bore into mine. The vampire king.

Chapter 26: The King

Previously:

I dive through the curtain between them and land inside the tent on my hands and knees.

The impact ripples up my stinging arm and into my head. I raise my gaze, resisting the urge to close my eyes from the headache.

Rahlan is staring at me in horror. My eyes are drawn to the man behind him. He has a long face, curly brown hair and a silver ring on his head that glows in the candlelight.

Two iron hands lock around my biceps and pull me to my feet. "My deepest apologies, King Groel," a guard says, "We did not foresee her second attempt."

His red eyes bore into mine. The vampire king.

The guards drag me back faster than I can walk. My feet trip over each other, putting all my body weight on my arms.

"Hold," the king commands.

The guards stop, allowing me to stand but not releasing my arms.

The king steps towards me.

"Pardon the interruption," Rahlan says, "My new pet is not yet trained."

I glare at him, and he shoots me a sharp look.

The king cups my chin in his cold hand, forcing my head up. I tug against the guards, but their fists are like stone. A vampire is touching my face, and I'm helpless to stop him. My neck and shoulders are completely exposed. I can't move an inch.

He finally removes his hand, but his gaze stays locked with mine. "Did the little one miss her master?"

I glance at Rahlan. He's not pleased. The king could order his guards to attack me, and Rahlan wouldn't be able to do anything to stop them. Not wanting to anger him, I give a small nod.

"'Tis pleasing to see humans dependent on their owners – the natural roll of their species," the king says.

Our natural roll? I turn my head to hide my expression. It doesn't matter what he thinks.

"Dismissed," the king says. The guards release my arms before exiting out the curtain behind me.

The king returns to his desk with Rahlan. I rub the numb spots on my arms, watching both of them.

"I heard that you were too eager to wait for the city gates to fall?" the king says, "Charging in alone again?"

"I couldn't risk the weasel Ivan slipping away," Rahlan says. He appears to have relaxed now that the king has lost interest in me. I guess the king can't execute a lord, but no such protection is afforded to a human like me.

"I take it he did not?" the king asks.

I pull my feet together and fiddle with my fingers.

"We will not be hearing of him again," Rahlan says.

They're just talking like I'm not here. I'm not seen as an enemy citizen who could leak their strategic information. I'm seen as a piece of property.

The king straightens the map on the desk. "I imagine it was cathartic?"

Rahlan folds his arms. "Why am I here?"

The king steps behind the table and brushes a sheet of paper off the map. "Your father's estate is in chaos – guards scattered, mob justice not uncommon. Your mother's not the leader he was."

"'Tis not surprising."

"I sent a liegeman to restore order, to act as a surrogate ruler. Your mother will continue to enjoy the luxuries of a lord's lady without the inconvenience of managing her lands."

"As she prefers."

"Now as I have done a favor for you, you must do a favor for me," the king says, "Become my vassal."

Rahlan's gaze falls onto the map stretched over the table. "My war with the humans is over."

"Great rewards await."

"My sword no longer strikes for silver."

The king's lips make a thin line. "If you will not fight, will you at least govern?" He points to the map.

Rahlan leans in. I want to see too, but I figure my presence is unwelcome.

"Litton Keep," the king says, "Taken from the humans a week ago, with its village in need of guidance."

Some human villages are allowed to remain? Though I'm guessing guidance is a euphemism for something much more sinister.

"'Tis far from the frontline. You will not be disturbed," the king continues.

Rahlan rests his chin in his hand. The king scrutinizes his expression, trying to read him.

"Okay," Rahlan agrees.

"Excellent." The king smiles. "I will have my servant bring you my letter."

Rahlan rests an arm on my shoulder and guides me out the tent. I glance back at the king as we pass through the curtain. His eyes remain focused on the map, with the small rubies in his silver crown shining in the candlelight.

I feel much better walking through the camp with Rahlan by my side. None of them will challenge me now, and it helps to lean my weight on him.

"It was just simpler to say I was your pet, right?" I ask, looking up at him.

He smirks.

"You got what you wanted, and like you said, your war with us is over. I'm leaving as soon as I can walk again."

He lifts me up onto the wagon. "Your taste has grown on me."

"Ha, ha," I spit, "I am not your cup."

He walks Mittens around to turn the wagon. "I'm confident that a little training will amend your rotten attitude."

I glare at him.

A young man hurries over to us. "Lord Rahlan?"

Rahlan nods, and the man hands him a short cylinder. "The king's letter."

Rahlan thanks him and climbs on the driver's bench.

Mittens hauls us out the camp, back onto the dark road. Heading away from that vampire hive allows me to relax again. I fold the blankets into a soft nest and snuggle between them.

Thin clouds drift across the starry sky above as we travel.

* * * * * * *

I sit up and stretch from my nap. The afternoon sun warms my skin. I slept most of the journey, and my body has thanked me for it. My head feels much better, only hurting if I put pressure on the wrong place.

The wagon crests a hill, and a castle comes into view. I grab the waterskin and take a seat next to Rahlan on the driver's bench. "Is that Litton?"

He nods.

The castle has tall stone walls, but it's nowhere near the size of the last city. Unlike Lord Guerin's former castle, this one has no mote.

Arrows lay embedded in parts of the wall too high to reach, and the wooden gates are stained with burns – remnants of a siege. This was a human castle not long ago. I hope the inhabitants managed to get away.

We enter through the arched gate, and Rahlan parks the wagon against the castle wall. A handful of guards on the ramparts watch our movements.

The castle's keep is situated on a small grass hill, and the walls form a perimeter around the hill's base. Unlike the cities before, there's not much inside. A modest tower built in the wall houses the guards, and a thin thatch roof protruding from the stone acts as a stable.

I hop off the wagon and stroke Mittens' nose. "That was far. Well done."

"No appreciation for the driver?" Rahlan says.

"The driver brought me here against my will."

"You're not particularly willing to go anywhere."

"That's because you kidna-"

"State your business." Two armored vampires stand before us. The black-haired one rests his hand on the hilt of his sword, making the blond-haired one look friendly by comparison.

I step back beside Mittens. Getting injured in a vampire skirmish would just be stupid.

"I am Lord Rahlan, vassal of King Groel, and new appointed governor of Litton." He hands them the small cylinder. The blond guard pops the lid open, and a rolled letter falls into his hand. He breaks the wax seal and unrolls it, his eyes scanning the page.

The black-haired one has a thin battle scar across his face. His mean eyes meet mine, and I quickly look away.

The blond one rolls up the letter again. "Welcome, Lord Rahlan. I am Julke, and this is Keld." He gestures to the other vampire who's finally taken his hand off his sword.

"And those are the Maksan twins." He points to two vampires on the wall. "We are the protectors of this keep. Our swords are at your service."

"Four men for the entire fort?" Rahlan says.

"The humans are in no state to counterattack, and the people of the village fear us," Julke says.

"'Tis not the humans that concern me."

What non-human force could he possibly have to worry about? The vampire's fury seems directed at my people alone.

Rahlan grabs my arm and tugs me to stand beside him. "This is my pet."

"Asshole," I mumble under my breath.

Keld shoots me a sharp look. I shift on my feet. What's his problem?

"My poorly mannered pet," he clarifies, "Arrest her if she tries to leave but go no further. I prefer to deal with such matters personally."

I yank my arm away.

"You have done well despite your numbers," Rahlan begins, "Close the gates. We're not welcoming any further visitors. You'll have to forgive me for our short introduction, but I have traveled far and am in need of rest. Tomorrow we will gather again."

The men nod and return to the gate. The thick wooden doors are pushed closed from either side, and a large wooden plank is laid across them. The men strain to lift it up and slot it in place. If two burly vampires struggle to operate the gate, then I have no chance of opening it on my own, let alone without anyone noticing.

Rahlan grabs his bag and frees Mittens from the wagon. His arm wraps around my shoulder and guides me up the short hill to the castle keep.

The old door screeches over the stone floor as he pushes it open.

He nudges me in ahead of him. "I introduce your new home."

I step inside the vast room. Large arches support the tall ceiling, and the high windows allow the setting sun inside, coloring the stone room orange.

My boot slips over some powder, and my gaze falls to my feet – blood.

Chapter 27: I'm Here

I leap away from the pool of blood. It's dry, and the streak leading towards the door suggests that the victim was dragged away well before we arrived. I doubt whoever stayed here would be allowed to live peacefully in the village. This may be all that remains of them above ground.

Rahlan closes the door and walks around the maroon patch. He steps onto the raised stone platform at the far end of the room. "First time inside a castle?" he asks.

I nod.

He gestures broadly around the room. "I present the main hall – for judging quarrels between peasants." His hand lands on a wooden chair with a high back. "This shall be my throne. If you're good, I may allow you to sit on my lap." He smirks.

"Thrones are for kings, my lord."

The smirk quickly fades. He presses open a set of double doors, and I follow after him. The doors close on their own behind us, assisted by gravity and their angled mounting.

"The living area," he says. A built-in fireplace surrounded by cushioned furniture fills one half of the large room, and the other half is occupied by a long stainwood table with eight matching chairs. A set of curtained windows overlook the castle gate. This room alone is as big as my entire house.

I step after him into a narrow passage lined with three doors. He opens one, and I peer inside. A large window shines orange light over a pristine wooden desk and matching bed.

"The servants' quarters," he says.

This was for a servant?

He continues down the passage. I hurry to press the doors open to glance in each room – all as beautifully furnished as the last.

We enter what appears to be a kitchen with wooden cabinets and limestone counters. Rahlan pulls back a line of thin doors in the wall, revealing the living room from before. "This is where you will prepare my meals."

"You'll love my veggie stew," I say.

His eyes narrow. I'll cook him as many vegetarian meals as his heart desires.

I return to the living room. A sparkle on the wall catches my attention. I creep closer and can hardly believe my eyes at the sight. A golden doorknob. It looks too valuable to touch.

Rahlan doesn't share my hesitation. He opens the door, breaking my trance. "The royal bedroom," he says.

I'm taken aback by the sight. The dim sunset passes through the stained-glass windows, lighting the room in a myriad of beautiful colors.

The bed looks fit for a king, with decorated thin posts in each corner to support a colorful canopy. I run my fingers over the elegant carvings in the posts. Dragons and knights dueling, their fire and swords embossed with gold in so much detail that I could search it for hours and still have more to discover. Jacob would've loved this.

I sit on the bed and run my fingers over the fine fabric.

Rahlan unpacks his bag onto the dressing table. My eyes follow his hands as he picks out each item – the sextant, the waterskin and my biscuit tin.

I grab the tin and press open the lid. The honey biscuit waits inside – my gift for Jacob. The gift he'll never receive.

He was going to be so impressed that I brought him a honey biscuit. He always used to bring me gifts from his travels, and I could never repay the favor. Now that I'd gone on my first long journey, I'd have something special for him.

He was never particularly excited for the meals I'd cook. Vegies weren't his favorite, so on Saturday's I'd take special effort to make him a vegie-free meal, whether that meant trading at the market for meat or churning butter for bread. He'd often try trick me into thinking it was Saturday on a weekday, hoping I'd cook one of his favorite dishes. I used to go along with it sometimes, just to see him try to hide his grin when he'd thought he'd gotten away with it.

I miss his mischievous smile. I wish more than anything that I could talk to him again, just to tell him how my day was. He'd listen to me complain about the farmer and the other workers for hours and never grow tired. Whenever I was sewing, he'd be so curious to know if I was making something for him. Silly. It was always for him.

A tear drops into the tin, and another one hits the biscuit. Who's going to listen to my stories about my day now? Who's going to travel for days to trade so I never go hungry? Who's going to comfort me on those rainy nights when I miss mom?

"You weren't saving it for yourself," Rahlan says.

I shake my head, barely able to regulate my breathing. The thought of eating it makes my stomach twist up in knots. It's Jacobs. Why did he have to die? I'd give up everything to have him back. I'd happily spend the rest of my life serving a vampire if it meant he'd have been spared. He didn't deserve this.

The bed sinks as Rahlan sits beside me. He rests his hand on my shoulder. "'Tis okay."

I shoot up and shove his hand away. "No! You don't get to say that!" I scream with a broken voice. "You murdered him, just like you murder every other human who gets in your way without any thought, without a care!"

He stands, but I hold my ground. "Yes. I ended your brother's life. I wanted to make all of them suffer as I had suffered."

"You belong in hell!" I scream at him, tears running down my cheeks. How could he do that? How can he be so content with the destruction he's caused?

He grabs my arm above the bandage, bringing my blurry gaze up to him. "Now I see, they do not suffer in death." He threads my hair behind my ear. "All I did was hurt the sweetest girl I've ever known."

Another sob escapes me. Whenever things were tough, Jacob was there to tell me it would be okay. As long as we're together, it would be okay.

Rahlan pulls me close and wraps his arms around me, holding me in his embrace. "I wish I could bring your brother back. I wish I could reverse the scars on your heart. I know that my words mean little to you now, but know that I truly am sorry."

I sob into his shirt. I shouldn't take comfort in Rahlan's hug, but I don't care anymore. It doesn't matter what is right or proper, what I should or shouldn't do. I just want this hole to go away.

Jacob's gone forever. I'll never see his smile or hear his laugh again. Everything would be okay if we were together, but we're not. We'll never be together again.

Rahlan's arms wrap tightly around my back, pressing me into him. Jacob hardly got time to live. He didn't get to see this beautiful castle. He would have been admiring every arch in the lord's hall, telling me the meaning of every piece of furniture and explaining how the golden dragons were embedded into the pillars. He should be here. He's the one who'd truly appreciate this place, not me.

Rahlan gently rocks back and forth, supporting my weight with his embrace.

* * * * * * * *

The sun is gone, and the room is dark. I don't know how long I cried for, but my face is warm and wet, and my back is sweating where my skin touches his.

I nudge away from him, and he releases me. My whole front half is warm, like I've been lying face down on a bed for hours.

He kneels to be at eye level with me. "I will be just outside the door," he says.

I nod, wiping my face.

He leaves the room, gently closing the door behind him.

I'm feeling a bit better now. I know I have to move forward without Jacob. After everything, I still have my life, and he wouldn't want me to wallow in sorrow forever. He was a good man.

I pull the corner of the stain glass window. It rolls into the wall, revealing a second layer of normal glass behind it. This room overlooks vast rows of grassy hills, dimly lit in the moonlight. Small thatch-roofed houses glow in the distance – Litton village, the place this castle was once built to protect.

The castle wall looked so much taller from the outside, but this hill elevates me above it, allowing me to look down upon the ramparts. The four vampire soldiers are nowhere to be seen. They must have moved inside the roofed towers as the night became cold.

I press open the door to the living room. The fire's lit, and Rahlan's shuffling around in the kitchen. I take a seat on the couch where the fire can warm my arms.

Rahlan sits beside me, handing me a steaming mug with a peculiar smell.

"Thanks," I whisper.

I take a sip and immediately regret it. My face scrunches up as the awful warm liquid coats my mouth. I wince and force myself to swallow the foul beverage, and the scratchy aftertaste makes me cough.

"What is this?" I ask, still not fully recovered. "It tastes like hot water mixed with herbs."

"It could be." He shrugs. "I'm not too familiar with your human cuisine."

He just mixed hot water with a bunch of random spices he found in the kitchen. The thought of him digging through a spice cabinet in confusion is amusing. At least he tried. I'll have to teach him how to make tea.

The mug warms my fingers. I'll dispose of it when he's not looking.

His gaze is on the fire, watching the flames lick the decorated metal.

"Rahlan, I've been wondering why."

His eyes land on me, and he raises an eyebrow.

"Why did..." I trail off, unsure of my words. "Why did you do it?"

"Your brother was a Huntsman," he says.

"But why do you hate them?"

He looks back at the fire. "Forget it."

He collected the eyes of the three men I was traveling with, so they must've been Huntsmen too. His hate for the Huntsmen is the reason I was captured, and it's the reason my brother died. It's everything.

"I just want to understand," I mumble.

"I said forget it." He stands, turning to leave.

How can he dismiss me for wanting to know why Jacob died? I jump to my feet. "Is it because the Huntsmen are brave enough to fight back? You only like humans small and weak like me, humans you can control?"

"No!" He whips around. "You stupid girl. They do not fight back. They are the Huntsmen. Hunters. They came into my father's land and slaughtered him in his own garden – an old graying man who had never wronged a human in his life. Is that brave? They mutilated his body, cutting out his eyes. Is that heroic? They carved 'monster' across his chest with a dagger. Does that encourage you to praise them further?"

I grab my own hands. That can't be. Ivan's not a killer. My brother's not a killer. They protect people. I take a step back.

The door slams shut, breaking my trance. Rahlan's closed himself in the bedroom.

There are many Huntsmen. Jacob couldn't have been involved. Sure, he acted tough when negotiating with strangers, but he was sweet, not the kind to sneak up on someone to murder them. How would he even know how to use a sword? He wouldn't be able to hide such a terrible deed from me, let alone live with it himself. It's impossible.

But Ivan's their leader. How could he have not known about an assassination by his own men? I remember him always being kind to me, but I was eleven the last time I saw him. I'm just fooling myself pretending that I know he's above something like that.

I hurry to the bedroom door, listening for any sound from Rahlan. The huntsman who escaped down the river called Rahlan a monster, and I called him a monster too. I knew it upset him, that's why I said it. He wasn't simply insulted. I was mocking his father's death. What kind of a person does something like that?

I knock my knuckles against the door, but there's no answer.

"Rahlan- Rahlan, I'm sorry."

Silence.

I try twist the golden doorknob, but it's locked. Pressing my ear against the wood reveals nothing. I slide down the door, still listening.

There's not a word, not a step on the floor, not a creak from the bed, nothing to indicate his presence.

I should never have said those words. I should never have pushed him. He shouldn't have to agonize because of my thoughtlessness.

"My mom died when I was thirteen," I say to the door, not knowing if he can hear me. "It hurt. I pushed everyone away. Despite that, my brother consoled me, and though I hated to admit it at the time, it helped. It helped a lot."

I pause for a moment, listening for any sound of him.

"Rahlan, I'm here. Don't push me away."

My head leans back against the door as I give up trying to listen for minute sounds. He's in there by himself, grief-stricken, because of my insensitive words. I curl my knees to my chest and huddle up to keep warm.

A latch clicks, and I jump to my feet. The door opens, and the firelight reveals that his eyes are misted over. He looks nothing like the man I've known for the past few weeks. There's no smug smirk or arrogant demeanor. He looks tired.

I take his hand in mine and tug him back to sit on the couch near the fire.

He watches the flames, his face expressionless, his gaze dull.

I lean my head against his side. All this time he's moved with such conviction, so sure of his actions every step of the way. He'd just convinced himself that making Ivan pay would make things better.

He lifts his arm, wrapping it around my side and pulling me close to him. I know he's my captor, but that doesn't mean I want him to be unhappy.

A log cracks in the fire, splitting into smaller pieces. I glance up at Rahlan. His head lays back against the couch with his eyes closed. He drove Mittens through the night while I slept. He needs rest.

Chapter 28: Bound Again

I sit up and rub the sleep out of my eyes. My body longs for the couch's warm fabric the moment I stand. Morning sunlight peeks through the windows, scattered by the curtains and making the white ashes in the fireplace sparkle. Rahlan is absent. He must've already woken up.

My dry mouth urges me to get a drink. I hesitate before touching the golden knob on the bedroom door. A strong chemical smell assaults my nostrils the moment I press it open. Rahlan's mixing potions on a desk with his back to me.

I step around him to grab the waterskin, careful not to disturb him before retreating out of the room.

"Sit," he says.

I stop at the door's threshold. His gaze hasn't moved off his work.

I take a seat on the bed, watching him as he pours two clear liquids into a gray mixture. He cuts a strip of linen off a large shirt belonging to the previous resident. Small bubbles form around the strip as it's submerged into the solution.

He kneels by my legs. It's odd not having to look up at him.

He begins peeling back the bandage around my arm, taking great care not to pull off any healing scabs around the wound.

A familiar smoky aroma fills the air as he lifts the new bandage out of the gray mixture. I stare at the long cut on my arm. This is my first time seeing it. It's not gaping open, but rather a thin red line, and it feels deeper than its surface level appearance.

I wince as he begins wrapping the soaked bandage around my fore-arm.

"Too tight," I gasp.

He grabs my wrist to keep me still. "'Tis necessary."

I grit my teeth and try to resist the instinct to pull away. He's a soldier. He's probably done this a thousand times before, whereas I've never dealt with anything worse than a minor gash. I should trust his judgement.

He finishes the tight wrapping, ending it with a knot. His eyes travel carefully up and down my arm, inspecting the skin beside the bandage. He's meticulous with his work.

After a few minutes, he seems satisfied enough to move on to the bandage around my chest. My gaze follows his hand as he picks at the knot that holds it all together.

I wrap my arms around my stomach. When this bandage comes off, I'll be topless in front of him. I know that he has to change it, and it would be stupid to risk attracting a disease over a little embarrassment, but I can't help but feel vulnerable under his eyes with the power he has over me. If he wanted to humiliate me, in front of the soldiers or just himself, I wouldn't be able to do anything to stop him.

The bandage loosens, and my arms shoot up to cover myself. He tugs the old material out, revealing the cut on my sternum. I keep my arms crossed tight over my chest, shielding myself from his eyes.

Bubbles form in the gray potion as he dips a cloth into the liquid. He leans closer with the damp material in hand, his eyes boring into my chest.

"It looks good," he says.

What?

I wince as he dabs the cloth over the cut. Oh.

He folds over a small piece of linen and presses it against the wound, then he threads another strip under and over my arms.

The bandage gets snagged on my elbow, slipping out of his hand. His lips form a thin line. I'm allowing no more than a tiny gap between my chest and arm for the linen to slot in place.

The bandage catches on my arm again, making him growl. "You realize that I've already dressed this wound once?"

"Don't remind me."

He slides the final piece of the bandage in place and terminates it with a knot. I let my arms fall away, glad to be covered again.

He takes a seat beside me, the bed sinking under his weight. His hands work to unwrap the bandage around my head.

He adjusts my posture to inspect the wound. I hope it doesn't look too bad. The terrible headache from before is gone, so it must be at least a little better. Despite him being partially responsible for these injuries, I'm grateful that he's here to look after them.

His hands slip under my legs and lift me onto his lap. The stubble on his chin brushes against my neck, warning me that he's about to take his drink.

I run my fingers over my hair that was covered by the linen. "Aren't you going to put another bandage on?"

"No need," he says. His teeth poke into me, and he begins syphoning.

This is the first time he's drank from me since the battle. I was hoping that it would be a permanent change, but I suppose he was just giving my body time to heal. At least this affirms my belief that I am indeed getting better.

He pinches the cut closed, holding me for a minute.

His hands latch onto my hips and push me to stand. The room spins for a second from rising so quickly, but he keeps his hold on me until I'm steady.

He packs up his potions and steps out the door. "Be at the table for breakfast in one hour," he says, leaving me alone in the room.

I grab the waterskin, collect some ash from the fireplace and head out the front door, careful to avoid the puddle of dried blood.

The bright morning sun warms my skin. The keep is situated on top of a small grassy hill, surrounded by the castle walls. The dirt footpath beneath my feet leads down the hill and splits into two. The one side connects to the stables against the wall where Mitten sleeps, and the other side attaches to the large wooden front gate, which is currently shut.

There's a platform over the gate and a tower beside it. A soldier is leaning against the tower's post – Keld, the scarred vampire with black hair. He's watching me.

I find a dry patch of grass and make myself comfortable, trying to ignore his menacing gaze. I'm pretty sure I'm allowed anywhere inside the walls anyway. If he tries to chase after me, I can just slip back inside the keep.

I brush my teeth with the water and ash, making up for the days I skipped when I was recovering from my headache.

My fingers scrunch up into a fist, flexing the muscles under the fresh bandage. Rahlan may be compassionate right now, but what would he do if he learned that Ivan's still alive? What would he do to me?

It's not safe for me here. The question is not if I will go, but where? Now that Jacob's gone, I have no family or friends, no one who'd welcome me.

I pick a long stalk from the grass and begin weaving it into a circle. That's not completely true. Ivan is my blood, regardless of how long it's been since I last saw him. But if he was easy to find, then Rahlan would have cut him down already. He was far better equipped to find Ivan then than I am now.

No. Rahlan may have had resources, but I have a connection to Ivan he never had. My brother was a Huntsman, a Huntsman who visited my uncle often.

I rack my mind trying to remember if he'd ever told me about Ivan's home.

Nothing jumps out. He never described the paths he took or landmarks he followed, and now that I think about it, he was even reluctant to point out his routes on his map. The emergency plan to reunite in Fekby village was the first time he even showed me a path on his map, and that was the last day I saw him.

I sigh and press my hands over my eyes.

Fekby village, of the Kingdom of Faria. He was insistent that I memorize the route, like he was worried that our home would be lost, and we'd need to reunite somewhere else. On the night we fled, I remember being overjoyed that Neil and his companions were also heading to Fekby. It seemed like a windfall at the time, that I wouldn't have to travel alone. But Rahlan wouldn't let them escape. He took their eyes, his ritual of revenge inflicted on every Huntsmen he kills.

Four Huntsmen all planning to meet in Fekby? It couldn't have been down to chance, that they all happened to pick the same random village. It's a Huntsmen sanctuary. That's where I'll find Ivan, or where I'll find someone who'll know his location.

But first I need to escape. In both my previous attempts, I had to make a desperate dash from Rahlan who was never more than a few yards away. There was no other option. I was tethered to him and every step north was a step deeper into danger. Now, I can scope out my environment and plan my route.

The large wooden doors are immediately out of the picture. They're sealed shut most of the time, needing two men to lift the large beam holding them closed. Plus there always seems to be a guard hovering around that area, watching the road leading to the gate. They'd spot me immediately.

I walk the perimeter around the castle keep, staying a good distance away from the walls so I can retreat inside if one of the vampires try to confront me. Five guard towers link the tall walls in an uneven pentagon. Each wall is in direct line of sight of two or three towers, and I can't see any way to get over them that doesn't involve going through one of the towers. Escape won't be easy.

The front door opens behind me.

"Breakfast awaits," Rahlan says.

I follow him inside. The table sports two plates of saucy mince surrounded by silver cutlery. I grab a piece of bread from the kitchen cabinet and take a seat across from him. Breaking the stiff bread in two reveals no mold. Whoever was living here was forced out not long ago.

My eyes land on the saucy mince on my plate. One of his potions must preserve meat, as there was no time to slaughter an animal this morning.

The salty sauce calls out to my empty stomach. Meat was usually reserved for Saturday dinners, requiring hours of preparation. This is a treat.

I scoop up the mince with the bread.

Rahlan snatches my arm, yanking my hand away from my mouth. The saucy bread lands back on my plate.

"What's wrong?" I ask. Did he spot something in the bread with his vampire senses?

He releases his grip. "No human of mine will dine like a barbarian."

A barbarian? Despite what he believes, he does not own me. I am my own person, regardless of if I'm free to roam the land or stuck in a prison cell.

"I am no human of yours," I hiss.

"My pet will not embarrass me with poor table etiquette. You will use the utensils provided." He gestures to the silver knife and fork.

"I am not your pet, and I will eat as I always have." I pick the bread out of the mince and take a bite.

He shoves my arm flat on the table. The bread flies from my hand and rolls across the stainwood, leaving a trail of sauce in its wake.

"You will dine with manners," he says.

I jump to my feet, my chair screeching against the stone floor. His grip on my arm prevents me from standing straight.

"You will remain in your seat." His stone hand keeps me trapped.

"Bite me."

"Later." He rises to his feet, and his red eyes darken. "Sit."

I gulp and take my place back on the chair. He releases my arm and circles behind me. I watch him from the corner of my eye, keeping my neck stiff.

He steps into the bedroom, leaving me in peace for the moment.

I tear off a new piece of bread, scoop up some mince and quickly munch it down.

The bedroom door slams shut with a bang, making me flinch. I jump upright at the sight of the rope, but his heavy hands land on my shoulders and force me back down onto the chair.

His cold maroon eyes meet mine, and I avert my gaze.

Realizing that I've resigned to sitting, his hands retract. He picks up the torn bread and brings it up to his face for inspection.

I thought we were done with this – him tying me up. I hate having my arms restricted. He's already twice my strength. Bindings aren't necessary for him to overpower me, but he chooses to tie me up regardless, almost as an insult.

"I was going to award you one more opportunity," he begins, "but it seems you squandered it the moment I left the room." The rope snaps straight between his hands like a whip.

Why should I sit here and endure his power trip? I try stand again, but his hand presses my back flush against the chair, applying some pressure to dissuade me from trying a third time.

He wraps the rope around my middle, making extra loops around my limbs to secure them to the chair's frame.

Satisfied that I'm immobilized, he returns to his seat and enjoys another forkful of mince.

I glare daggers at him.

"You will remain in your seat until you've mastered proper table etiquette," he says without looking up.

The knife in his right hand scoops the meat onto the fork in his left. He doesn't pay any attention to me or my death stare. I'm hungry, and my meal is sitting just a foot away from me, so close I can smell it, but completely out of reach.

He finishes his food and takes his plate to the kitchen to wash. I hope it slips out of his hands and shatters on the floor.

He returns and takes a seat on the table beside my untouched plate.

"Ready to try again?" he says.

I hold his stare. He can go make love to a cow.

"Suit yourself." He hops off the table and heads outside.

I wiggle my shoulders from side to side to try get free, but the rope just allows my hands to slide up and down the backrest without loosening at all. It's wrapped around each of my wrists and the chair's frame, allowing me to bend my arms as much as I want but keeping my hands functionally useless.

My ankles are tied to the chair legs in the same way. I can bend my knees up to my chest, but the rope just slides up and down the wood, keeping my ankles rooted to its frame. A strut between the legs makes slipping my feet under the posts impossible.

The stupid pigheaded narcissistic vampire has me trapped.

Chapter 29: Submission

The sun is creeping through the west windows. I've been stuck on this chair the whole day while the mince mocks me with its mouth-watering scent. Beautiful carvings decorate the chair's bulky frame to which I'm bound. Like everything in this castle, it's built with high-quality workmanship which would've carried an equally high price. It's constructed to last, making it annoyingly sturdy and impossible to break with the strength in my limbs.

The door opens, and Rahlan steps inside. He sits on the table and gently moves the blonde hair out of my eyes. "Ready to reconsider your position?"

I want to bite his finger, but that may give him the excuse to bite me back with his sharper teeth. Fighting him got me tied up, reaffirming that he can just do whatever he wants to me. He claims he's now keeping me as his pet – a demeaning term for a human kept close to quench their captor's thirst for blood, though that's a role I've been forced into since the day he got me.

I nod, wanting nothing more to be done with all of this.

"Good girl."

He makes my blood boil.

The rope around my wrists and ankles falls away as he loosens the knot. I stand and stretch, taking a walk around the room to get my blood flowing again.

He turns the chair, its wooden frame grinding against the stone floor. I don't have the stamina to continue fighting over his stupid eating customs.

I take a seat back on the chair. He pushes it to bring me closer to my plate.

I pick up the fork.

"Wrong hand," he growls.

I swap the fork to my left hand and take the knife in my right. I don't have any practice performing the precise movements to scoop up food with my left hand. Why bother trying to use two tools at once when I could hold the food better with my right?

The bread is the largest item on my plate, making it my first target. If I get my first few bites right, then maybe he'll lose interest and let me eat the mince in peace.

I stab the bread with my fork and bring the large piece up to my mouth. It's too big to eat in one go. I nibble a small bit off the side while trying to keep the bread from falling back on the plate.

"Cut it first," he says, his tone indicating that it's not a request.

I lower the bread back to the plate, afraid that ignoring his command would anger him and get me tied up again.

Handling the oddly-shaped knife and the fork at the same time proves to be too much of a challenge. I push the bread off the utensil and opt to try the mince. My wobbly hand struggles to keep the fork steady as I raise the saucy meat up to my mouth. Keeping it level proves difficult, and soon all the mince has fallen back on the plate.

I try a second time but only succeed in bringing an empty fork up to my mouth. On my third attempt some of the saucy meat hits the table too.

"Stop it," he snaps.

"Both refusing to use the fork and trying my best to use it sets you off," I say.

"Your best?" He moves closer, his proximity like a heavy weight on my shoulders.

I frown. I try using his ridiculous cutlery, and he accuses me of deliberately being difficult so he has an excuse to tie me up again. I was bound to the chair for hours thinking it was because of my choices, that if I'd just submitted to him then he wouldn't have snapped.

I meet his gaze again. "You make it impossible for me to succeed so when I fail you can punish me under the pretense of justice. If you want to punish me then just do it. You're my owner as you say. I can't stop you. But don't try trick me into believing that if I submitted to you that I would've been spared from your wrath."

I hide my face from him, afraid that my tough expression will soon break. It's hurtful to be manipulated like that.

He rests his hand on my shoulder. "Binding you did not bring me joy."

I keep my gaze on the ground, unwilling to look him in the eye. "Fooled me."

"How am I to persuade you to do as I ask without the incentive of discipline?"

"Aren't Lord's meant to be leaders?" I doubt he treats his soldiers like this. "Being your captive doesn't make me any less of a person."

He takes his hand off my shoulder and rests his chin on his knuckles.

"I prepared this meal, so you agree that it belongs to me?" he says.

I nod. He can keep it. None of this was worth a plate of food.

"I will gift you this dinner if you consume it with proper table etiquette."

"Thanks." I push the chair back and head for the passage attaching to the servant's quarters – a place which offers nothing more than a peaceful environment. He doesn't move to stop me like before. I'm not thanking him for effectively taking away my meal, but for giving me a choice.

"You are not hungry?" he asks.

I stop at the threshold. "I tried your table etiquette. It wasn't good enough for you."

"I misjudged the situation. Return and I will teach you with patience."

The mince's salty aroma lingers in the air. The sun hangs low in the sky, and I doubt he'll let me out to forage this late.

I head back to the table, but he takes my seat before I can.

"Sit." He pats his lap.

My lips make a thin line. I'm not a child.

He catches my arm and pulls me closer. His hands snap to my middle and lift me onto his lap, pressing my back against his chest. He holds my fingers in his. "I will guide you."

My left hand is lifted with his, and he curls my fingers around the fork. He does the same with the knife in my right, keeping his hands on mine to hold them steady. He directs my movements to scoop some ground meat onto the fork and brings it up to my mouth, keeping the utensil steady.

I open up, and he relaxes his hold. I take a bite, completing the last of the motion myself. Even cold, the mince is delicious, boasting a wonderful texture and a sweet aftertaste. Having beef would be a treat on its own, but these must be some of the best cuts.

He guides my hands through the motion again and again, giving me a little more control each time. By the end of the meal, my left hand can hold the fork more-or-less steady if I concentrate.

He lifts me off him and takes the plate to be cleaned. I sneak down the passage before he demands something else.

I wander through the servants' quarters with only a few lonely streaks of dim moonlight to guide me. I can't hear any trace of Rahlan's presence in here, making it hard to believe that these rooms are still part of the same massive building. I'd hate to live alone in such a large and creepy home. You'd never know if an intruder was sneaking around in the middle of the night.

I search through a chest in a servant's old room. An uneasiness hovers over me, but I know just as I will not return to the ruins of my village, these people will not return to their castle. Rahlan probably considers all this his property now anyway.

A sparkle from a needle leads me to a sewing kit, and searching a little longer yields some leftover leather pieces too. These are exactly what I need to fix my tunic.

The bed creaks as I lay my weight on it. The room is silent. The moonlight provides nothing more than an eerie glow, leaving half the room pitch black. My gaze lingers on the dark void. Anything could be there, and I wouldn't know.

I rummage through the chest in search of a candle. My hands feel for a waxy texture but come up empty. I grab the sewing kit and head back to the living room, stopping right at the threshold.

Rahlan has lit the fireplace. He's reading a book on the couch. I remain in the shadows, not letting myself be seen. The warm fire and cozy couch look inviting, but the presence of a vampire makes me wary. This is his home now. His couch. His fire. I'm out of place.

He turns a page in his book. "You are welcome here, Julia."

Chapter 30: His Lap

I jump at his voice.

How did he know I was watching? I was as silent as a mouse. He didn't even glance in my direction.

I step out of the shadows and grab my torn tunic from the kitchen counter. He's on the left side of the couch, so I take a seat as far right as I can. I'm not joining him because I want to be near him, but because he's the only other person in this creepy building.

He glances at me before returning to his book. I'm welcome here – beside a vampire, on his furniture. He's a soldier of a foreign army, and he wants me in his home. I never imagined being in this position, living with a vampire.

Running my fingers through the tunic reveals a long cut on the right sleeve and a small hole in the chest area, matching my own injuries. I thread the needle and begin with the sleeve. Sewing a crisscross pattern, the two sides are pulled together as I go.

The fire burns a perfect distance away, enough to keep me warm, but not too much to be uncomfortable. Soon the hole is sealed, but it'll need some reinforcement if I want it to last. I flip the sleeve inside out and attach a leather patch over the cut. It'll strengthen the area while being invisible from the outside.

Satisfied with my work, I thread my arm through the sleeve and give the repaired area a few tugs to make sure it holds.

"Let me see," Rahlan says.

I pass the tunic to him, and he inspects the repaired area.

"'Tis like new," he says with a puzzled expression.

"I made clothes whenever there was spare linen. We couldn't afford to buy from a tailor."

"You need not worry about that again." He speaks as if I'll be trapped under him for the rest of my life.

The fire radiates its heat over me, and my body sinks into the couch. I run my fingers over the small hole in the middle of the tunic, deciding where to start.

Rahlan turns a page. His book is bound in leather and lined with silver thread. The golden title glints in the firelight, drawing my eyes to symbols too complex for me to decipher.

"What are you reading?" I ask.

"'Tis a story about a prince that falls in love with a princess, but he's forbidden from marrying her," he says.

"What happens?"

He smiles. "I've only begun reading."

"Will you read it to me?" I always loved when Jacob would tell the stories he'd heard from those he'd met on his travels.

"That'll slow me down. You'll need to do something in return."

My lips make a thin line. What is he planning?

He puts the book aside and pats his lap. "Lay here."

"No." I cross my arms and slide as far away as the couch allows.

"Suit yourself." He opens the book again.

I watch his eyes jump back and forth as he finishes each line. Not a minute later, he's trying to suppress a laugh. There's comedy too?

I slide over to him.

His lips curl into a smirk. He places the book on the table beside the couch, making room on his lap.

"You better read from the beginning." I lay my head on his legs, facing away from him.

He rests his hand on my side, his soft touch surprising me.

I push the hand away. The agreement was only to lay on his lap.

He clears his throat and turns to the first page. "Harris sprinted through the field, leaving a trail of broken stems in his wake. The seeds and dust stuck to his sweaty brow. He needed to reach the homestead before they found out – or more specifically, before his mother found out."

The fire's warmth makes my eyes scratchy. They drift closed, and I nestle into the soft couch. Rahlan caresses me as he reads, his hand trailing from my shoulder to my hip. I'd swat him off, but though I don't want to admit it, it's soothing, making my limbs heavier than stone.

* * * * * * *

Something moving my body brings me back. My scratchy eyes blink open before sealing shut again. Rahlan's carrying me. I let my head loll back in his arms, too exhausted to readjust myself.

He lays me down on a cool material. Peeking at my surroundings reveals the bed's fabric glowing blue in the moonlight. I twist onto my side and ball my fists up in the blanket, embracing it. Feathers plump up the soft pillows, and the sheets are smooth like silk.

My boots are pulled off my feet, exposing my toes to the cold air. He unclips my belt and slides the stiff leather pants off my legs. I don't mind sleeping beside him in my underwear. This wouldn't be the first time.

The bed shifts beside me, and I'm engulfed in his arms. The feeling of his cold skin shocks me at first, but I soon adjust as he begins to warm.

The fine sheets and plumy pillows hug my frame, whisking me away.

* * * * * * *

I rub the sleep out of my eyes, bringing the room into focus. The bed's four pillars support a canopy embroidered with beautiful images of mountains, rivers and sheep. The sun's rays are beginning to peek through the drape covered windows, brightening the room.

Rahlan's arm is around my middle. It's warm. He's always warm in the mornings despite feeling cold the night before, sort of like a blanket.

He slides me on top of his chest. I try sit up, but the hands on my back keep me pressed against him. My body isn't awake enough to struggle.

His nose creeps to the base of my neck. "Prepared?" he asks.

"Mmhmm," I mumble.

He bites his favorite spot. I lay limp on top of him. My whole body is raised with each breath he takes. I'd imagine it would be uncomfortable for him, but he doesn't appear bothered. I weigh little compared to his strength.

His fingers pinch the wound until it's healed.

He nudges me off him. I sit on the side of the bed, scratching my head. The curtains are swept aside, allowing the bright sunlight to flood the room.

My eyes follow Rahlan's muscular frame as he walks. It's unusual to see him half undressed. Even in sleep he'd wear his shirt, but I suppose he doesn't need it for warmth now that he has thick blankets and an insulated stone bedroom.

He opens the wardrobe, the action causing the muscles on his back to form ridges. That's why he can pin me to a chair with one hand. How would he feel if we magically swapped places, if I was the one who could overpower him with one arm? I bet he wouldn't be so arrogant then.

"Which do you prefer?" He holds out two dresses – one dark purple with fine thread that reflects the sun and the other a sky blue with white frills on the sleeves.

"The purple makes your eyes pop," I say.

His eyes narrow for a moment before he tosses the purple dress to me. "Then that will show everyone who you belong to," he says.

I run the fine fabric through my fingers. The threads are packed so tight that I can barely tell them apart. These are clothes of a noblewoman, meant for lavish banquets and balls. "I'll stick with my leather armor," I say, "And what did you mean by everyone?"

He tightens the belt around his waist and ties his shirt. "Your tunic is repaired?" he asks, ignoring my question.

"Almost." The chest still has a hole from his sword.

"My pet cannot be poorly dressed." He slides his coat over his shoulders. "It would not serve well as a first impression."

"First impression? Who are we meeting?" I ask, brushing off the pet comment.

His curved sword slides into the sheath on his belt with a click. "I have a village to subjugate."